Adopting Faith:
The Truth About Libby

Adopting Faith:
The Truth About Libby

By Julie Eckert

ISBN: 979-8-218-08820-0

Editing and interior layout design by Kevin Miller - www.kevinmillerxi.com
Cover design by Sumwhatsouth Creative - www.sumwhatsouth.com

Published by Lily of the Valley Publishing
email: publishing@mylilyofthevalley.org
www.mylilyofthevalley.org

CONTENTS

Dedication   7
Acknowledgements   9
Chapter One   11
Chapter Two   21
Chapter Three   31
Chapter Four   43
Chapter Five   55
Chapter Six   65
Chapter Seven   73
Chapter Eight   81
Chapter Nine   89
Chapter Ten   95
Chapter Eleven   101
Chapter Twelve   107
Chapter Thirteen   111

DEDICATION

I wish to dedicate this book to my grandchildren, Rayce, Emersyn, Hailey, Ben, and Ethan. Follow the Lord with all of your heart, soul, mind, and strength for this is Life and He will guide you in your steps.

ACKNOWLEDGEMENTS

I want to thank my husband, Mike, for always being supportive of my "projects." I want to thank those who took the time to read the book and give me constructive feedback on improvement. I want to thank my Lord and Savior for laying this book topic and words on my heart. I know not the reason why, but I know God has a plan and for that, I will trust Him. I want to thank Lily of the Valley Publishing for being supportive and faithful to a calling placed on them by God.

CHAPTER
ONE

Libby could no longer stop the tears from flowing. Her heart was completely broken, her dreams shattered.

Her greatest fear? That she would never heal. She lay across her bed, wondering if she would ever have the strength or the desire to get up. It seemed as if time was standing still, and death had come knocking.

How could this have happened, and why? If only she would have gone with him or begged him not to go. If only she would have answered his call, he might still be there. So many "what ifs," but none of them could bring him back. It all seemed so surreal.

Exhausted from the grief, she fell into a deep sleep, and her dreams began, or so she thought.

It was dark, and Libby was unsure of her surroundings. She could see the moon shining through the trees and fog rolling across the meadow. She was lying on the ground, her clothes moist from the dew. Slowly, she arose, still dazed and confused. Feeling pain in her head, she put her palm up against her left temple. As the memory of the past three days came crashing back into her mind, she slouched to the ground, sobbing so hard that her entire body shook, the painful memories sweeping over her in waves.

It seemed as though hours had passed before she was able to stand up again. She looked around, trying to identify her surroundings, how she may have gotten there, and why she was in such a strange place. She took a cautious step forward, followed by another. Then, without hesitation, she ran past the edge of the woods and into a clearing.

The moon was full and shining brightly, as if a light switch had flipped on in the night sky. Turning in a full circle, she looked for something, anything that would help her understand where she was or why she was there.

As Libby stumbled forward, she sensed a heaviness that would not lift, the weight of it so oppressive that she felt as if it could crush the breath out of her. She tried to shake the feeling as her mind reeled with jumbled thoughts.

The grass beneath her feet was soft and wet, causing her to realize she was barefoot. Why would she be outside in such a strange place with no shoes? Her situation seemed so mysterious and awkward. Rain was falling gently, and the fragrance of flowers wafted up into her nostrils. How could such sweetness enter the bitterness growing in her heart? Would the bitterness take hold or dissipate under the dread that was consuming her? Libby's mind drifted back to the only thought that kept her from yielding her mind and body to the growing doubt and fear: Brian.

Brian was the one person whom Libby had felt a close connection to since her parents died. In the few short months that they were together, Libby felt a strong and enduring tenderness, growing into what she felt could be a lasting relationship. Their friendship was just beginning to blossom into a budding romance that seemed like a fairy tale, a dream come true. After her parents died, meeting Brian was the only good thing in her life. Libby had been tossed from one abusive and dysfunctional foster home to the next. Her parents were killed in a house fire when she was only ten years old. How was a ten-year-old supposed to live a happy, normal life without her parents?

Libby was at a slumber party when the fire took her parents' lives. The party was a last-minute invite from her friend, Melissa. Libby and Melissa had known each other for a while but had only recently become good friends. Her parents encouraged her to go, so she excitedly gathered up her overnight bag with her pajamas and a few games. She had never been to a slumber party and was a little anxious. Would the girls like her? Would she miss her parents and be homesick? Her parents assured her that if she became homesick that she could call, and they would come to get her right-away. Libby loved her parents immensely, though she felt an unusual sense of trepidation. She was looking forward to the new adventure.

Melissa lived in a two-story Tudor-style home. It was large and stately with four bedrooms, each with its own ensuite. The main floor had a large foyer with a dining room on one side and an office on the other. Melissa's father sold insurance and worked from home most of the time. With the office so close to the front door, he would have clients come there when needed. There was a kitchen just off the dining room with a massive island and commercial stove and refrigerator. The foyer opened into a sunken living room with a wall of windows leading to the back patio and pool area. A hallway to the right led to a half bath and the master bedroom on one side and a game room on the other.

The girls were to bunk in the game room with sleeping bags on the floor. Melissa had invited several girls to her party. It was probably the biggest party of the year, and all the girls chattered about it at school. Libby was unsure why her invite was last minute, but she embraced the opportunity. Melissa lived across town from Libby in a subdivision called Turtle Creek. The neighborhood was teeming with children, something Libby was not used to. She was an only child and spent much of her time with her parents and their acquaintances. The only time outside of school that she spent any amount of time with children was at church.

At around seven in the evening, Libby's parents dropped her off at Melissa's, once again assuring her that they would come if she needed them and that, if not, they would see her early the next day.

"Let the party begin," Libby said, grinning as she hugged and kissed her parents, then she hopped out of the car. As she reached the front door she turned and waved one last time. As her parents drove away, her mother blew her one last kiss, which Libby pretended to catch in her hand. Her father tooted the horn as they rounded the corner and then disappeared from sight. Libby entered the house, met by the laughter and chatter of several girls.

There was not much slumber at the slumber party. The girls had a blast dancing to the songs of their favorite singers, eating pizza, and playing board games when they were too tired to dance anymore. They chattered noisily about school and boy crushes. Libby was pleased that her parents had encouraged her to come. Being an only child, she didn't get to experience the excitement and craziness that came from having siblings.

As the night started to wind down, they put in a movie that Mrs. Killian streamed on Netflix. It was a new movie called *Princess Christina and the Fairy Monster.* The girls quieted down as the movie began.

Once it was over, they tucked themselves into their sleeping bags, and Mrs. Killian turned the lights out.

In the dark, one of the girls told a joke, which started a cascade of giggling that went on until around 2:30 a.m. when the girls finally quieted down enough for them to fall asleep. Libby dozed off with such joy in her heart, yet a chord of discontent echoed there as well. She shook it off and, as she drifted off into a blissful sleep, vowed that in the future she would go to more slumber parties.

The phone rang early the next morning. Mrs. Killian had just gotten up and was preparing to make a huge pile of pancakes for the girls. She had already put on a pot of coffee for Mr. Killian, as neither of them had slept much.

"Hello and good morning," she said. Moments later, she gasped, causing Mr. Killian to raise his head from the morning paper. "Oh no," she said. "Of course. I'll have her up and waiting for you."

Mrs. Killian hung up and then turned to her husband in disbelief, tears welling in her eyes. How could this have happened, and what would it mean for Libby? She explained the content of the call to Mr. Killian. Then she crept into the game room where the girls were sleeping and gently shook Libby awake. "Come, dear, you need to get up."

Libby rubbed her eyes, then got up and tiptoed out of the room. Mrs. Killian quietly closed the door behind them and then led Libby toward the living room. It was still quite early, and Libby was uncertain why Mrs. Killian had woken her. She thought that perhaps her parents had missed her, so they were there to pick her up early.

As they entered the living room, the doorbell rang. Mr. Killian opened the door to an attractive young woman with a smile that would put anyone at ease. Mrs. Killian invited her in and asked her if she wanted a cup of coffee, then sent Mr. Killian to retrieve it. The young woman sat on the couch and then invited Libby to do the same, patting the spot next to her. Libby glanced at Mrs. Killian, who encouraged her to sit. With some hesitation, Libby went to the couch and sat down.

"Hi, Libby," the young woman said. "My name is Nancy McCord, and I'm a social worker from child welfare."

Libby was confused. Why should this matter to her, and what could Nancy want with her?

"Libby," Nancy continued, choosing her words carefully, "there's been an accident at your home, and I'm sorry to have to tell you that both of your parents have been killed."

In an instant, Libby's head was spinning, and she felt sick to her stomach, as if she were going to vomit. She turned to Mrs. Killian, who was sitting on the other side of Libby, imploring with her eyes for understanding as she struggled to wrap her mind around what she had been told. "My mom and dad are coming to pick me up in a little bit," Libby exclaimed. "We're going to the Blue River to ride the canoes. My daddy promised, and he does not break his promises to me." The look in Mrs. Killian's eyes told Libby that that was never going to happen.

Mrs. Killian teared up as she pulled Libby into a hug. Libby fell into Mrs. Killian's arms, the realization of what was happening hitting her hard. After sobbing for a few minutes, she pulled away from Mrs. Killian's grasp and looked at Nancy. "What happened to my parents?"

Nancy took Libby's hands and explained that, at around midnight, a fire broke out at her home, and the smoke and fumes overcame her parents. They succumbed before they could make it out of the house. The neighbor's barking dog woke them, alerting them to the fire, and they called 911. When the firefighters arrived, the home was engulfed in flames, preventing them from entering the house or doing anything to save her parents.

Libby didn't remember much of the conversation after that, as she collapsed back into Mrs. Killian's arms and sobbed some more. It would be years before Libby would come to understand the truth behind the fire, that truth adding one more insult to her tragic young life.

The funeral was a blur to Libby. As she sat in the pew at the back of the church and watched people walk through the line one by one, greeted by Mrs. Killian, her thoughts drifted to memories of her parents.

"What color of flowers do you think we should put in the window boxes?" her mom queried.

"The red and yellow ones," Libby replied. "I think Daddy really likes those colors."

Libby loved going to the plant nursery with her mother. Each spring they would plant flowers in the window boxes on the front of the house and along the walk up to the entryway. Libby picked out Forget Me Nots and yellow Jasmines to put into the window boxes. Along the walk, she chose an array of perennial flowers. Her mother would always remark that Libby had a real flair for pairing different colors and species of flowers. The local newspaper had even featured pictures of their home in the garden section, which made Libby incredibly proud. Although she wanted to grow up and run the family business, she also felt a desire to work in a plant nursery. Her mother told her that they would have plenty of time to figure out such things and for her to enjoy being a child for now. Libby squirmed in her seat as the realization hit her once again that they would never get to have that conversation.

Raised in a small town in Midwest Indiana, Libby loved camping out in her backyard and riding her bike throughout the neighborhood. They lived on a cul-de-sac in an older but modest Victorian home. Long before she was born, Libby's parents bought the home and spent the next few years painstakingly refurbishing each room. Her mother took a lot of time to plan the colors and furniture and wall-paper patterns that she would use to bring back the flair of the era in which the home was built.

Her parents owned a small hardware store in town, so her father got most of the supplies at cost. They had new water pipes and wiring put in first for safety. Then they put in sheetrock and painted the walls and ceilings. Her mother spent hours varnishing the woodwork throughout the house, which was just over 4,000 square feet divided into three levels.

The main floor consisted of a formal sitting and dining room, a half-bath, a kitchen, and a solarium, which was situated on the backside of the house. Her mother made the solarium into a reading nook surrounded by plants and potted flowers. Through the French doors, off the solarium, was a garden with a large white arbor at the end of a stone path. The second floor consisted of a master bedroom with an ensuite bath and two other bedrooms adjoined by a full bath. The third floor was a loft with a full bath. Each room had the original windows, which extended nearly from floor to ceiling, filling them with a tremendous amount of light.

Initially, the loft was used for storage until Libby was born.

Then her mother converted it into a playroom. It had a huge bay window with a window bench on the far end of the loft. During the day, sunlight would fill the loft, and Libby would often sit on the window bench soaking up the sun. At night she would lie on the window bench looking up in the sky, counting her blessings as she counted the stars. As Libby grew older, she dreamed that one day she would convert the loft into her own private getaway. Now all of her plans seemed like a frivolous waste of time.

"I'm so sorry for your loss, Libby," a woman's voice said. Drawn out of her deep thought, Libby looked up to see Mrs. Miller, her fourth-grade teacher. She hugged Libby and then gave her a small locket in which she had placed a picture of Libby's parents on one side and a picture of Libby on the other. She remarked on how beautiful the service was and how proud Libby's parents would be of her.

Libby agreed that her pastor, along with Mr. and Mrs. Killian, had done a wonderful job of the funeral arrangements. The flowers were gorgeous, and their fragrance filled the church, reminding Libby of all the trips to the nursery with her mom. Mr. and Mrs. Killian had thought it best to have the funeral at the church because Libby felt comfortable being there, her parents having spent many years serving in the church.

Libby walked toward the caskets, stopping to touch and smell the variety of flowers that lined the aisle, each flower representing a special memory of her parents. When she reached the front of the church, she sat on the stool placed next to the caskets for her. The fire had done extensive damage to her parents' bodies, so the caskets were closed. An eight-by-ten picture of her parents sat on a table between the caskets.

Mrs. Killian stood next to Libby as many more people filed past, pausing to hug and talk with Libby about her parents. Many of them spoke of how Libby's parents beamed as they talked about her and how much they loved her. At times Libby would have to step away to collect herself. Because Libby's parents owned a local hardware store, many of the people who came through the line were unfamiliar to her. Libby had no immediate family, as both sets of grandparents were deceased. She was a late-in-life child and an only child, as were her parents. She never stopped to consider what this would mean for her, but she would soon find out.

It was hard for Libby to grasp that her parents were gone. She half expected them to come walking in and take her back home. Each time the church door opened, her heart leapt in anticipation of something that was impossible.

The day was exhausting for Libby. The funeral service had started early that morning with visitation followed by a sermon at 10:00 a.m. As much as she wanted the day to end, she was also dreading its conclusion, as it meant saying goodbye to her parents forever.

Once everyone had filtered out of the church at the end of the service, the pallbearers carried the caskets to a waiting hearse. The ride to the cemetery was short. Once there, the pastor spoke at the graveside, saying that Libby's parents would rise again someday because of their faith in Christ. This brought hope to her even though she didn't understand how it could happen.

As the caskets lowered into the ground, Mrs. Killian gave Libby a yellow-and-red rose to lay on each one. The scene played out as if it were a movie that Libby was watching rather than an event she was actually experiencing. She rode with Mr. and Mrs. Killian back to the church for a meal prepared by the women of the church. Libby watched as people sat around eating and memorializing her parents. All she wanted to do was go home and head to the loft, her special place of solace.   But Libby would not be going back home ever. With no immediate family to care for her, Libby would be going into foster care. The lot where her home once majestically sat and the hardware store, both of which were eventually sold, provided money put into trust for Libby until she turned twenty-one years of age, which seemed as if it was a lifetime away.

CHAPTER
TWO

Libby's first foster home felt normal enough for a while. Her foster parents, Mr. and Mrs. Ward, were an older couple who had been fostering children for many years. They lived in an upscale neighborhood in a four-bedroom home with three full baths. They figured they had room for up to six foster children at a time. Not many children stayed for longer than a few months, but they did have two children who had been with them for over a year.

One of them, Macy, was eleven years old and was eager to have a new sister in the house. Her long, flowing blonde hair was pulled up into a ponytail, and her blue eyes twinkled when she smiled. She was tall and thin for her age but agile and full of spunk. She volunteered right away to have Libby stay in her bedroom, which faced the back of the home. Their room overlooked a large back-yard filled with jungle gyms and a trampoline. A privacy fence surrounded the yard, which also contained a small pool.

The second child, Eli, was only eight and had been with the Wards for close to two years. He was a handsome brown-eyed boy with curly brown hair and a sweet, naïve disposition. The minute he saw Libby, he ran up to her with a big smile, reveal-ing his missing two front teeth. He gave her his best bear hug. The Wards planned to adopt both Eli and Macy, and after meet-ing them, it wasn't hard to understand why. Both children were loving and lovable.

A few weeks after Libby's arrival, another foster child came into the home. His placement was not supposed to be long. The goal was for him to be there until the foster family who had planned to take him returned from vacation. His name was Matt, and his demeanor was downtrodden and menacing. At age thirteen, he had a stocky build and looked more like a young man. His brown hair hung just below his shoulders, and he wore it with a side part that drooped over his eyes most of the time.

After Matt arrived, things began to change around the home. He entered the foster-care system because his mother overdosed on a mixture of drugs and alcohol and died. His father was found culpable for her death and was sent to prison. Both of Matt's parents were into drugs, and many nights he would come home to find them strung out and high. When he arrived home the night his mother died, his parents were sitting in the living room smoking marijuana and drinking highballs. Matt didn't notice the tourniquet and syringe on the coffee table as he hurried through the room, hoping to avoid having to speak to his dad. He had never seen either of his parents shoot up drugs in the past. Matt's father had brought home a new drug for them to try. He said a guy who he worked with had recommended it and had even offered to give him a couple of doses for free. Matt's father didn't object. Who would turn down a free high?

Their home was small and usually a mess, with empty whiskey bottles and old pizza boxes sitting on the coffee table and the kitchen bar. His mom was not much of a housekeeper, but when sober, she would joke around with Matt and call him her little Mattie Pie. She would hug him as she tousled his hair. That always made him feel special. Matt knew that both of his parents had issues, but in his heart he blamed his father. He was the one who had always brought the booze and drugs into the home. If not for him, Matt's mother would have had more time for Matt and not been strung out most of the time.

Coming home and seeing them at it again, Matt headed to his room and did what he always did when they were high: put on his headphones and fell asleep to the music. Matt had gotten into the habit of listening to rap music that typically incited hate speech and misbehavior. He would drift off to sleep thinking about how he wished he could kill his dad so that he could have his mother's attention all to himself again. So much hate and bitterness was buried in his young heart.

The next morning when his dad woke, he jumped out of bed and yelled for his wife to get up. He had forgotten to set the alarm again and was late for work. His boss had warned him the past week that if he were late again, he would be fired. He didn't take the time to reach over and make sure his wife was awake. He showered, dressed, and rushed out the door, cursing the entire time.

The cursing woke Matt, and he rolled out of bed. He had not even bothered to change into his pajamas the night before. He got up, stretched, and looked out the window. It was a dreary day, rainy and a little cool. A good day to stay in bed and sleep. He used the restroom, washed his hands and face, brushed his teeth, then headed for the kitchen. He thought he was alone and didn't realize that his mother was still in bed. Matt's parents were usually gone by the time that he got up for school. When his dad remembered, he would leave Matt some lunch money on the kitchen counter. On the days that he forgot, Matt would either dig something up from home to eat or else borrow money from one of his friends. That day, he didn't feel like doing either. In fact, he decided he wasn't going to go to school at all. Instead, he turned on the television and sprawled out on the couch. If his parents didn't care, then why should he? After about thirty minutes, he fell asleep again to the drone of the television.

Matt had often been in trouble at school. His teacher sent notes home with him, but his parents would make excuses for Matt's behavior, and nothing ever changed. He was failing his classes, and his teacher feared that he was becoming a delinquent. Matt had also stolen cigarettes and drinks a few times from the Huck's store. The local police department had begun to develop a file on him, not that his parents cared.

Matt was drawn out of his sleep by the phone ringing. He almost didn't answer, believing it to be the school calling to leave a message that he was absent. He dragged himself off the couch to answer it. It was his mom's boss, yelling that if she didn't get to work within the next thirty minutes, she could kiss her job goodbye. Losing her job would infuriate his father. They were barely making ends meet as it was.

Figuring he would find her in bed hungover, Matt walked to his parents' bedroom and opened the door.

"Mom, your boss is on the phone," he said. As he reached the edge of the bed, he realized her face was pale and bluish. He reached down to shake her, then recoiled. Her body was cold and stiff.

Matt backed out of the room, hung up on her boss, then called his dad. Initially, his dad was angry that Matt had called him at work. His boss was already on the warpath because he was late again. Matt told his dad that something was wrong with his mom, but his dad told Matt to go back into the bedroom and put her on the phone. Matt tried to explain, but his dad just became angrier and threatened to beat him when he got home if he didn't put his mom on the phone. Matt carried the phone with him into the bedroom and slowly approached the bed. He could tell that she was not breathing and that her lips were blue. Matt began yelling into the phone. "Mom is dead! Mom is dead!" He hung up on his father and then called 911. Through his numbness, he was able to give them his address. Then his young mind slipped into a state of shock, and he wandered back into the living room.

Matt's dad asked a coworker to cover for him, then jumped into his truck to head home. He was furious with Matt and swore he would beat the daylights out of him for lying. If he lost his job over this, Matt was going to pay with his hide.

By the time Matt's dad arrived, the coroner and the police were already there. The police had confiscated the syringes and a bag of a powdered substance that they assumed was an illicit drug. Matt was sitting on the couch, too stunned to cry. He was still holding the remote in his hand after turning the television off when he called the police.

The coroner pronounced his mom deceased at the scene. Shortly after Matt's dad arrived, he was in handcuffs being escorted out to the police car. One of the officers asked Matt if he had any relatives. Still in shock, Matt just shook his head, so he was also escorted to a police car, which would take him to the station until child protective services came to pick him up. When Matt was finally able to feel and process the pain, his numbness turned to anger, and his anger turned to hate.

Matt was taken to a shelter to await a proper placement. The funeral was a blur. With his dad in jail, his grandmother was notified for the funeral arrangements. She didn't have much of a relationship with her daughter and had stored up years of hurt herself. She didn't have a lot of money, either, living on a fixed income, so she could not afford a proper funeral. Instead, she opted for cremation and a graveside service without a viewing. Matt was devastated that he was not going to get to see his mother one last time. Without that closure, his anger turned from his dad to his grandmother. How could she do such a thing and not even ask his opinion? As the pain and anguish piled up on him, the only way he could escape was to bury it and his head into his music, which filled his mind with more hateful lyrics that only influenced delinquency.

At the trial, it didn't take long for the jury to convict Matt's dad of involuntary manslaughter. With his history of drug and alcohol arrests, it didn't look good for him. Matt became a ward of the state and was placed into the foster-care system.

The day Matt arrived at Libby's foster home, the household had been busy preparing a room for him. Since his stay would only be a couple of weeks, he would room with Eli across the hall from Libby and Macy's room.

Matt came into the home defiant and angry. He demanded to know where his room was and then stormed into bed with his headphones on, shutting out the family. The social worker stayed for another thirty minutes to explain the circumstances surrounding Matt and that he was there because his grandmother refused to take him. His grandmother stated that he was probably trouble, like his parents, and she didn't want any trouble in her home. She never forgave her daughter for marrying a drug addict and felt that only bad seed could come from that union.

The Wards were empathetic toward Matt and gave him a wide berth even though his behavior was bad. He was only supposed to be there for a couple of weeks, so they didn't even attempt to discipline him, as they would have disciplined any other child who behaved similarly.

A few days after Matt arrived at the home, Libby was lying on the roof outside of her bedroom window.

She would often climb out the dormer window in her room

and onto the roof. She would lie there looking up at the stars and remembering the nights she would lie on the loft window bench at her home contemplating her future or the backyard camping trips she would do with her parents. Her dad would point out the big and little dippers and show her how to locate Orion's belt and many other constellations. Her mom would make s'mores as they sat around the campfire, singing songs that she had learned at vacation Bible school. The memories warmed her heart yet hurt at the same time because she missed her parents so much.

While on the roof that night, she heard an unfamiliar noise below. She crept toward the edge of the roof and peered over, spotting Matt sneaking into the basement window. It was around midnight, and Libby wondered why Matt would be out so late. She didn't want to ask or even let him know that she was aware that he had been gone. She feared that he would retaliate against her, as it didn't take much to anger him. Instead, she laid back down on the roof and, within a few minutes, fell fast asleep dreaming about her parents. She didn't rouse until she felt raindrops on her face. By the time she crawled back into bed, it was 2:00 a.m. She gave no more thought to Matt.

When Libby arrived home after school the next day, a police car was parked in the driveway. Just seeing the car brought back memories of her parents' death. When she entered the house, she saw a social worker and a police officer in the front room. Seeing them there, she feared the worst, as the last time she had seen such a sight was after her parents' death as she was removed from the Killians' home, never to return to her own home again.

The police officer was questioning Mrs. Ward and Matt. The officer asked Matt where he had been the previous evening. Matt said he had gone to the mall but then came home at around 10:00 p.m. and went straight to bed. Mrs. Ward verified that Matt was indeed home and in bed, unaware that he had snuck back out later that night. Libby then heard something that left her mortified. Matt's grandmother was murdered during the night, sometime between 11:00 p.m. and 1:00 a.m. The police said an intruder had entered through her bedroom window on the main floor and then beat her to death with a baseball bat.

Matt's grandmother lived about two miles outside of town on a small piece of property. She had never really been a part of Matt's life because she didn't approve of the way his parents lived. The few times that she had any contact with Matt turned into a huge fight between her and his parents, with Matt in the middle. Even so, after the shock of his mother's death and the anger over the cremation wore off, he longed to live with his grandmother rather than in a foster home, but she had rejected him, along with his parents. The pain he felt at her rejection ran almost as deep into his soul as the pain he felt at losing his mom. Libby wished so much that she had had a grandparent to live with, so she could understand Matt's pain. For a moment she almost forgot that Matt was an angry and frightening boy and felt a tinge of sadness for him.

When she heard about how Matt's grandmother had been brutally murdered, Libby gasped, drawing the attention of those standing in the front room. The police officer called her into the room to ask if she was OK. "I think that I am ok", Libby stammered, "I was just a bit surprised to hear about the murder of Matt's grandmother." Libby glanced at Matt, and he gave her a look that warned her that she had better not speak. Libby was sure that Matt had not seen her peering over the roof the night before, but she wondered if he might have investigated her room and noticed that she was not in her bed. He knew that she often went out onto the roof to escape into her own little world. Did Matt suspect that she had seen him sneak back into the house?

Instead of answering the police officer, she turned and raced upstairs to her bedroom. Several minutes later, Matt stuck his head through her bedroom door. "Snitches die," he warned. Then he walked away as Mrs. Ward came upstairs.

"Libby are you OK?" Mrs. Ward asked. All Libby could hear were Matt's words resonating in her mind: *Snitches die.* She slowly turned to face Mrs. Ward.

"I don't feel well. I feel sick to my stomach." With that, Libby rushed to the bathroom and began to vomit, mostly out of fear. Afterwards, Mrs. Ward helped her wash up, put on her pajamas, and get into bed. Then Mrs. Ward went back downstairs.

The police and the social worker were long gone. Matt's foster family had returned from vacation, and he was supposed to leave in the morning. Libby kept telling herself that he would soon be gone, and she would no longer have to worry about him.

However, that night she slept with her door locked and a chair wedged under the doorknob.

She opened the window a few inches to allow the wind to blow across her face. It was hard to fall asleep as Libby imagined Matt killing his grandmother. How could anyone do such an awful thing, much less to their own grandmother? Soon, however, fatigue overtook her, and she fell into a deep sleep.

Suddenly, Libby awoke. She heard a strange noise but could not place where the sound had come from. She glanced over at Macy, but she was sound asleep oblivious to any sounds. As Libby lay in her bed, motionless, she scanned the room until her gaze came to rest on the open window. The moon was high and bright, and within seconds it cast the shadow of a figure across the room. Someone was standing on the roof outside of Libby's bedroom window.

As the figure bent down and attempted to open the window wider, Libby held her breath, thankful that the windows had safety latches on them to prevent them from opening more than a few inches from the outside. As she lay there, frozen in fear, she heard cursing and thought she recognized Matt's voice. Several minutes later, the figure gave up and left. Libby didn't sleep for the remainder of the night. Why was Matt trying to get into her room? Was he planning to kill her like he had killed his grandmother to prevent Libby from revealing his secret? The thought sent shivers down her spine. Libby vowed to stay in her room the next day until Matt was gone.

When Macy woke up, Libby sent her downstairs to tell Mrs. Ward that she was going to hang out in her room and not to worry about her not having breakfast. Libby was fearful to run into Matt but also afraid that if she tried to eat anything, as anxious as she was, that she would become sick at her stomach.

Libby could hardly wait for the social worker to come and take Matt away. She stayed in her room, pacing, a sick feeling in her gut. It was another hour before she heard a car in the driveway. For a moment, Libby felt a sense of relief. Matt would soon be leaving her life forever.

She heard them talking below but could not hear what was being said, and she was not about to unlock her door and open it to listen for fear he would be waiting outside. *No,* she thought,

I'm not unlocking my door until I see them drive away with Matt in the backseat.

A few moments later, she heard the car engine start. She ran to peek out the window. As the car pulled away, she saw Matt in the backseat looking up at her with an evil grin on his face, which sent more shivers rippling down Libby's spine. Her relief that he was gone lasted only a few moments, for when she opened her bedroom door, she found a note taped to it that read: "I know you'll miss me, but I promise you'll see me again!" As she read those words, Libby was sick with fear.

Libby remained in a state of fear for most of the day until Mrs. Ward explained that Matt's new foster home was in a neighboring county, over twenty miles away. Libby took comfort in that because Matt was too young to drive, and it was too far for him to walk or ride his bike.

After Matt had been gone a few weeks, Libby willed herself to forget him and his grandmother's murder. The police kept the Wards informed about the case, but without any new evidence or leads, they were at a loss. Libby was still too scared to come forward with what she knew. Each time she considered doing so, she could hear Matt saying, "Snitches die." Libby had no reason to believe that Matt would not harm her, especially considering what she believed he had done to his grandmother. It was better not to tell, Libby reasoned, and the investigation into the death of Matt's grandmother turned cold, never to be solved.

Libby stayed with the Wards for three years. There was talk of adoption, but after long nights of discussion, Mr. and Mrs. Ward felt that they could only afford to adopt two children, Macy and Eli. Once their decision was made, they decided they would no longer foster other children, choosing to focus on raising Macy and Eli instead. Libby was scheduled to go to another foster home a few counties in the opposite direction of Matt's foster home, putting even more distance between them. She moved during the summer, so she could start high school at the beginning of a new school year. Libby was sad and hurt at having to leave the Wards' home, but she tried her best to understand their situation. She was happy for Macy and Eli but struggled with the fact that the Wards could so easily let her go. After a tearful goodbye, Libby moved in with a new foster family, the Pikes.

CHAPTER
THREE

The Pikes were new to the foster-care system, and Libby was only the second child they had taken into their home. Two weeks earlier they had accepted a nine-year-old boy named Adam. He was quite rambunctious and kept Mrs. Pike on her toes. Adam had lived a hard life, but despite that, he was happy and well adjusted. Adam's mother, Tracy, had been a runaway and a single parent. Raped at age seventeen, she chose not to give up her child. From the moment she laid eyes on Adam, she fell in love with him. She had some concerns about how she would feel raising the child of a man who could be so brutal toward another human being, but she didn't believe in abortion. With the help of a crisis center, temporary housing, and counseling, Tracy was able to complete a two-year degree, find a job, and make a home in a one-bedroom apartment for her and Adam. She did her best to provide for him. They didn't always have a lot of food, new clothes, or toys for Adam to play with, but they had an overabundance of love.

Adam had just turned nine when Tracy was diagnosed with stage-four ovarian cancer. Because they didn't have adequate insurance, she didn't seek medical treatment when she first noticed that she was having some abnormal symptoms. Her main concern was making sure that she had enough money to pay for Adam's care. By the time she sought medical attention for herself, the cancer was widespread and her condition terminal. Tracy handled the diagnosis with grace, her only concern being Adam's well-being. She met with social services and talked about the type of home she felt Adam would thrive in. The social worker assured Tracey that she would see to it that Adam was placed in a good home with a loving family.

Once Tracy felt assured that Adam would be cared for properly, she spent the remainder of her life focused only on him. Within two months of her diagnosis, Tracy succumbed to the cancer and died. Up until her death, she and Adam continued to laugh and love each other. She talked to Adam about where he would go after her death and that he had to be a good boy no matter where he was or whom he lived with. Adam promised he would always be a good boy. Adam was a happy and healthy but overly active young boy.

In hopes of running off some of his excess energy, Mrs. Pike enrolled Adam in a local park and recreation program. He spent the mornings swimming, playing, and doing arts and crafts. Adam would come home excited and chattering about his day, showing off his artwork, which Mrs. Pike happily displayed on the refrigerator. At the supper table, Mr. Pike would encourage Adam to sit still and eat, but he was so excited that he could not seem to comply with Mr. Pike's request. Mr. Pike tried to stay calm, but Libby could sense that he was seething with anger regarding Adam's behavior. Mrs. Pike thought it was cute to see Adam so excited and, without meaning to, encouraged him to keep talking despite Mr. Pike's request, further agitating her husband. He had only agreed to take foster children because his wife had begged and worn him down. They had found out two years earlier that Mrs. Pike was unable to get pregnant due to twisted fallopian tubes, but she desperately wanted to have children. Mr. Pike didn't care whether they had any children because he felt children were just additional mouths to feed and bodies to clothe. He enjoyed being the center of his wife's world and having the freedom to spend money on himself or go on vacation anytime he wanted. The only reason he had agreed to foster care was the revelation that a monthly check would accompany each child they took into their home. He was lulled by the extra money and what he could do for himself with it.

After a week of scolding Adam at the table, Mr. Pike was regretting his decision to allow Mrs. Pike to foster children. One evening at supper, he announced that he had decided that he would take Adam out to his workshop after supper to work off some of his energy. He told Mrs. Pike that he wanted to teach Adam how to do woodwork and that they would start small by making a birdhouse. This pleased Mrs. Pike, who was getting fearful that Mr. Pike was regretting his decision to allow her to foster children.

Adam was excited at the prospect of building a birdhouse, which only increased his chattering. Initially, he could not wait until supper was over, so they could head out to the workshop. He would gulp down his meal and impatiently wait for Mr. Pike to finish eating. As soon as Mr. Pike put his fork down, Adam was out of his seat and headed for the door. While Adam and Mr. Pike were in the workshop, Libby and Mrs. Pike would clean up and do the dishes. After about a week of going to the workshop every evening after supper, however, Adam's behavior began to change. He became unusually quiet and sullen.

The following week at park and recreation, one of the girls who worked with Adam, named Kathy, noted that he was quiet and seemed to withdraw when it came time for a swim, which was unusual for him.

He loved to swim and was usually the first one in line when it was time to go. Adam told her that he didn't feel well and preferred to stay at the shelter house and make crafts with some of the disabled children. At first, Kathy didn't think much about it, but after the third day, she came up behind Adam and put her arm around his shoulders, planning to talk with him about the change in his behavior. Adam winced at her touch. Kathy withdrew her arm as Adam looked up at her, somewhat sheepishly.

"Are you OK Adam?" Kathy asked.

Adam nodded hesitantly. "I fell out of a tree last night and hurt my shoulder."

"May I take a look at it?" she replied.

Adam shook his head. "Mrs. Pike looked at it last night and said it was just bruised but that I would be fine."

Kathy thought no more about it and encouraged Adam to be more careful when climbing trees. He went back to crafts as Kathy continued checking on and praising the work of each child.

Mrs. Pike arrived at the park at around noon to pick up Adam. Kathy approached her to let her know that Adam was still in pain from his fall out of the tree the previous evening. Bewildered, Mrs. Pike turned to Adam with a questioning look. Adam appeared embarrassed.

"I fell out of a tree last night and hurt my shoulder," he said.

"Why didn't you tell me, Adam?" Mrs. Pike asked. At bath time the night before, Adam had refused to allow Mrs. Pike to help him get ready, so she had not had a chance to see his back and shoulders.

"I was afraid I would get into trouble for climbing the tree." Mrs. Pike and Kathy seemed satisfied with his response. However, Mrs. Pike asked him to pull up his shirt, so she could see the injury. Both women were very concerned by what they saw. Adam had a large welt and dark bruises across his entire upper back. It looked as if he had hit many tree limbs on the way out of the tree. Kathy suggested that Mrs. Pike take him to see his physician to be sure there were no broken bones. Mrs. Pike agreed, and she and Adam left the park. That was the last time Kathy ever saw Adam and Mrs. Pike.

With the start of the new school year, Libby noticed that Adam sat at the back of the school bus alone and away from the other children. She thought that perhaps some of the older boys had been picking on Adam, so she sat next to him. Adam looked up at Libby with the saddest eyes she had ever seen on a child other than her own after her parents died. Over the past few months, Adam had gone from a bubbly, vibrant, chattering nine-year-old to a quiet, lonely, and withdrawn child. Concerned, Libby questioned Adam.

"What's wrong? Why aren't you sitting with your friends? Is someone picking on you?"

Adam sat quietly for a moment offering a one-word answer: "No." Libby decided to push a little harder.

"Adam, if someone is picking on you, we need to let Mr. and Mrs. Pike know. They don't want us to be bullied by other children, and they will put a stop to it." Adam became visibly upset and begged Libby not to say anything to Mr. Pike. Confused by his reaction, Libby agreed not to mention it. Instead, she told

Adam that if things didn't get better over the next week or two, she would have to tell a teacher. Adam was fine with that, as it gave him time to work out a new story.

When they got off the bus, Adam ran straight to his room, right past Mrs. Pike, without saying a word. As he reached the top of the steps, he turned to face Libby and mouthed, "You promised!"

At supper, Adam sat quietly as the conversation revolved around the upcoming school semester. Libby was looking forward to shopping at the mall, as Mrs. Pike promised that they could get some new clothing and supplies. Libby could not wait to look for cute clothes and shoes. She talked about the backpack that she wanted, and Mrs. Pike said she might even get a new laptop if she were lucky, grinning as she said it. Mr. Pike cringed at the thought of spending any money on the children. He had plans for those checks coming in, and those plans didn't include new clothes and a laptop. In Libby's excitement, she didn't notice that Adam just sat in silence, staring at his plate.

Once they completed the meal, the conversation began to slow. Mr. Pike asked Adam if he was ready to go to the workshop. Adam said that he didn't feel well and that he wanted to go to his room, but Mr. Pike would not allow it. He said that Adam was so close to finishing his project that he wanted him to see it through. With that, he and Adam headed for the back door. Adam was reluctant and moved slowly.

As Mrs. Pike and Libby picked up the dishes and headed for the kitchen, Libby felt bad for Adam. She thought that Mr. Pike should have let Adam go to his room if he didn't feel well. As she glanced back, she thought that she saw Mr. Pike grab Adam by the neck and shove him toward the door, jerking Adam's head painfully. *What was that all about?* Libby thought.

While doing the dishes, Mrs. Pike and Libby began to discuss the change in Adam's behavior. Libby thought about telling Mrs. Pike what she had just witnessed, but after her experience with Matt, she was fearful of making waves. Mrs. Pike had made Adam's favorite dessert, and she invited Libby to take some to the workshop for Mr. Pike and Adam in an effort to cheer him up. Libby eagerly agreed. It made her feel better knowing that she was doing something nice for Adam, especially since she wasn't willing to tell what she thought she had seen Mr. Pike do to him.

She dished up two brownies and covered them liberally with ice cream, chocolate sauce, and whipped cream. Then she headed out the back door with a huge grin on her face, imagining Adam's reaction to his favorite dessert. He would be so happy.

As Libby made her way through the backyard to the workshop, she could hear the radio and wondered why it was up so loud. As she arrived at the door, she discovered it was locked. She kicked it gently with her foot, her hands occupied with the desserts. When no one answered, she assumed they could not hear her because of the radio.

She walked around to the side of the workshop to peek through the window. The shutters were only cracked about an inch, but when she faced the window straight on, she could see into the workshop. Libby expected to see Adam and Mr. Pike putting the finishing touches on the birdhouse. Instead, what she saw caused her to drop both plates as her hands flew up to cover her mouth. Then she turned and ran to the back door.

At the sound of the dessert plates breaking on the concrete, Mr. Pike turned the radio down and listened. He made his way to the shop door to look outside. By the time he unlocked the door, Libby was back inside. He stuck his head out but saw nothing because the broken plates were around the corner of the workshop out of sight. He turned and shut the door behind him, locking it again.

Libby ran into the kitchen, her face red and her hands still shaking. Had she really seen what she thought she had seen? It made sense after the way Mr. Pike had grabbed Adam's neck earlier, but the reality was hard for her to face. She had not spoken up earlier but knew that now she had no choice.

Mrs. Pike noticed how distraught Libby was and asked her what had happened. She could not imagine what could have caused Libby to react in such a way. She sat Libby down in one of the kitchen chairs and handed her a glass of water, but Libby's hands were still shaking so badly that she could not take the glass. Mrs. Pike put the glass down and then began stroking Libby's back to calm her. Libby burst into tears, afraid that Mrs. Pike would not believe her but knowing she had to tell for Adam's sake. She drew a deep breath and began to speak, relaying as accurately as possible what she had seen in the workshop.

Recounting the story made her shake even more. Remembering what she had seen on Adam's back earlier, Mrs. Pike picked up the phone and called the foster child hotline to speak with a social worker.

Within the hour, a social worker and two police officers were at the house. After Adam's supposed fall from the tree, Mrs. Pike had approached Mr. Pike about Adam's injury. She had grown somewhat suspicious of Mr. Pike's behavior, and his answer didn't satisfy her, so she asked him if he had hurt Adam. Mrs. Pike knew deep in her heart that Mr. Pike had not wanted children and that the only reason he agreed to take in foster children was to keep her from moping around the house. After her accusation, Mr. Pike told her that she was crazy and a little paranoid, then brushed her off. "Little boys Adam's age are clumsy," he said. "He fell out of the tree while we were measuring a spot to place the birdhouse." At the time, his answer made sense, but she was uncomfortable with it. She still felt that Mr. Pike was not being honest, but she had no proof, and Adam was not saying anything. She opted to wait and see if anything further occurred. After hearing what Libby had seen, she knew she could no longer. She didn't realize that the social worker was obligated to contact the police.

When he saw two cars in the driveway, Mr. Pike told Adam to stay put, slapped him on the back of his head to let him know he meant business, then headed for the house. As he rounded the corner into the living room, everyone quit talking and looked up at him.

"What's going on here?" he asked.

Officer Harker asked Mr. Pike to take a seat and then asked him where Adam was. Mr. Pike refused to sit and said that Adam was in the workshop completing his birdhouse. Officer Harker summoned Officer Neal to retrieve Adam. Mr. Pike started for the door, saying he would get Adam himself, but Officer Harker stopped him in his tracks. Mr. Pike insisted again, but Officer Harker forced him to sit while Officer Neal headed out to the workshop.

Mr. Pike shifted nervously in his seat. Looking at his wife, he felt a loathing for her, knowing she was the one who had brought this trouble upon him. He glared at her, but she avoided his eyes, knowing what this could mean for their marriage, which was already strained.

When Officer Neal entered the workshop, he found Adam stooped to the floor and heard him whimpering.

"I'm not crying!" Adam shouted as soon as he heard the door. He kept his face turned away, fearful he would receive another slap if Mr. Pike saw the tears in his eyes.

Appalled at what he was seeing, Officer Neal knelt next to Adam, whose hands were bound. "Adam, my name is Officer Neal. I'm here to help you." Adam turned to look at the officer. The moment he saw the compassion in his eyes, he felt safe. Officer Neal could see a bruise starting to develop on Adams' cheek.

"Where is Mr. Pike?" Adam asked, his eyes narrowing in suspicion.

"He's in the house, son. Now let's get you untied and out of this workshop." After untying Adams' hands, they headed toward the house. Adam knew that this time he could not lie his way out of his injuries.

As those in the house waited for Officer Neal to return with Adam, Libby sat quietly, avoiding eye contact with Mr. Pike as well. Suddenly, Mrs. Pike began yelling at him.

"How could you do this? He's just a little boy!"

Officer Harker calmed Mrs. Pike, so the social worker could question Libby about what she had witnessed in the workshop. Libby was hesitant to answer with Mr. Pike in the room, so Officer Harker suggested that Mr. Pike wait in his bedroom.

"Both of those kids are nothing but trouble!" Mr. Pike roared as he stood up. "This one has a vivid imagination, telling all sorts of made-up stories," he said, pointing at Libby, "and that boy is nothing but a clumsy clown, falling and getting hurt all the time!"

When Mr. Pike was finally in his bedroom, the door shut, Libby began to speak. She was not quite sure how to describe what she had seen. However, her lips trembling as she wiped away her tears, she explained how she had been unable to get anyone to answer the door, so she headed toward the window. Just as she was about to explain what she had seen through the window, she began to whimper and cringe. In a calm and reassuring voice, the social worker urged her to continue. Libby drew a deep breath and then recounted what she had witnessed. "I saw Adam, his arms wrapped around the center pole in the room. Until Mr. Pike stepped away from him, I didn't realize Adam's hands were tied around the pole. He was crying as Mr. Pike yelled at him to shut up, or he would give him a real reason to cry. While Adam was trying to stop crying, Mr. Pike picked up a belt and swung it hard across Adam's back and then across his lower legs. He buckled and fell clumsily because he was tied to the pole. It was then that I dropped the dessert plates and ran back to the house."

As she was finishing her story, Officer Neal entered with Adam. There was a glimmer of fear in Adam's eyes as he dropped his head and slowed his pace. Officer Neal gently maneuvered him toward the others.

The social worker took one look at Adam and then stood up to meet him. Mrs. Pike shrieked as her hands flew over her mouth, and she began to cry. Adam's face was bruised and swollen from Mr. Pike slapping the back of his head while Adam was tied to the pole, causing his face to hit the pole. The social worker asked Adam if she could look at his back. He was afraid at first, but she assured him that it would be OK. He hesitantly turned his back toward her, so she could lift his shirt. His back was beginning to show new welts from the belt. When Adam realized that Mr. Pike was not in the room, he began to sob as the social worker cradled him. As his sobs abated, Officer Harker explained to Mrs. Pike that both children would be removed from the home for safety reasons while they completed an investigation and that Mr. Pike would be taken into custody for questioning. At that statement, they heard the bedroom door lock click.

Officer Harker headed toward the bedroom and knocked, ordering Mr. Pike to open the door. Mr. Pike would not answer, which concerned Officer Harker. He asked Mrs. Pike if she had a key to get into the room. She ran to the den to grab the key, which Mr. Pike kept on a hook by his desk.

As she returned, they heard a loud "pop." Officers Harker and Neal, familiar with the sound, drew their guns and went into a defensive stance, demanding that everyone get into the kitchen where they would be safer. The officers once again demanded that Mr. Pike open the door. When they received no response, they moved closer, identifying themselves once again before unlocking it with the key Mrs. Pike had provided.

When they entered the room, they saw Mr. Pike's legs sticking out from the opposite side of the bed and suspected the worst. As they rounded the bed with their guns still drawn, they saw the body of Mr. Pike, blood beginning to pool around his head. Officer Neal holstered his gun and bent down to check for a pulse. Finding none, he began doing CPR as Officer Harker radioed for an ambulance. They could see one gunshot wound to Mr. Pike's left temple.

Unable to wait any longer, Mrs. Pike came to the bedroom door. She entered the room and then collapsed at the feet of her husband's body, sobbing uncontrollably. Before the social worker could contain them, Adam and Libby rushed to the room, the social worker hot on their heels. They watched the disturbing sight unfold until the social worker whisked them both away, stunned and speechless.

Officer Harker helped Mrs. Pike to her feet and escorted her to the couch. She was inconsolable as she recalled her last words to her husband. They were hateful words, seething with accusations, the last words she would ever get to speak to him. She began to blame herself for what Mr. Pike had done and then turned her anger onto the children, blaming them. If only she had discounted the story Libby had shared with her and not called the social worker. If only she had not said those hateful words. If only . . . The social worker took the children into the kitchen where she asked them to remain as she went back into the living room to try and comfort Mrs. Pike. Alone in the kitchen, Adam began to cry again. Libby scooted her chair next to his and held him in her arms.

"I hope he's dead," Adam said. Libby's heart broke to hear him, at such a young and tender age, say that he wanted anyone dead. She could only imagine the pain that Adam had endured at Mr. Pike's hands, so didn't try to dissuade him. She just let him cry and vent all the anger that his nine-year-old heart felt.

Minutes later they heard an ambulance siren, followed by the hustle and bustle of the paramedics bursting through the front door. Even though it was apparent that Mr. Pike would likely not survive, they began resuscitative efforts as they secured him on the gurney and headed toward the door.

They had to pause before they reached the door because Mrs. Pike ran to his side and held him as tightly as she could, sobbing. The older paramedic, Sam, explained to Mrs. Pike that they needed to get him to the hospital as quickly as possible for advanced life support. Begrudgingly she let go of the gurney as they whisked Mr. Pike out of the house and secured him into the back of the ambulance. Sam climbed into the back with Mr. Pike as the younger paramedic drove the ambulance to the hospital, sirens blaring the whole way.

Officer Harker offered Mrs. Pike a lift to the hospital as the social worker prepared to take the children to a temporary site for the night. The children didn't even have a chance to say goodbye to Mrs. Pike before she was in the back of the police cruiser and gone.

In the back of the ambulance, Sam provided basic life support as his partner radioed ahead regarding the grim situation and their estimated time of arrival.

Mr. Pike was declared dead on arrival. The emergency room doctor allowed Mrs. Pike the time that she needed with her husband to grieve. An hour later she was at the police station answering questions, her mind swimming.

Libby and Adam were taken to a shelter, where they stayed the night. The next day they were sent to two separate foster homes. The only time the children saw each other again was at the trial for Mrs. Pike, who was arrested shortly after Mr. Pike's death because the social worker believed that Mrs. Pike was complicit in her husband's abuse of Adam and didn't report it. Had she reported it sooner, Mr. Pike might still be alive. As part of the trial, the children had to testify, not before a court or in Mrs. Pike's presence but in the chambers of Judge Nichols. He was an older man with salt-and-pepper hair and a mustache. He had gentle eyes that immediately won their trust. He allowed them to tell the story in their own words, assuring them that they were in no trouble.

Mrs. Pike was found guilty of not reporting the abuse and was sentenced to three years, but her sentence was reduced to house arrest with time served, partly because of her testimony against her husband and because she, by calling the police that night, probably saved Adam's life. Her hopes of ever fostering another child were dashed as her license to foster children was revoked.

Mr. Pike was buried two months prior to the trial. However, a note that he had scribbled was later found under the nightstand. He had overheard the conversation that was taking place in his living room and knew he would be going to jail. Child abusers didn't fare well in jail, so he would be facing bullying of the worst kind by the guards and the inmates. He would likely be tortured and murdered in prison and figured that if he were going to die, it would be on his own terms. Therefore, without remorse, he pulled the trigger to save himself from the same type of abuse that he had inflicted on Adam.

The formerly rambunctious nine-year-old was never the same after his experience with Mr. Pike. Adam went to a very good foster home that eventually adopted him, but he spent the next two decades in therapy. He grew to be an angry, suspicious, spiteful man. A repeated theme of his therapy sessions focused on him blaming Libby and Mrs. Pike for allowing the abuse. He was angry that he was the one who had been abused and not Libby. In many of his sessions, he made veiled threats against them both.

CHAPTER
FOUR

Libby was not as fortunate as Adam had been when placed in her next foster home. Her new foster home already had five biological children, and Libby was the fifth foster child.

The Thompsons owned an eighty-acre farm that had been in Mr. Thompson's family for several generations. The farmhouse was an old plantation-style home built in 1870. It was a large home with five bedrooms and a servants' quarters. Although it had been a grand home at one point in history, the lack of care and upkeep had caused it to sag and peel. The kitchen had a large pantry and a back staircase to the servants' quarters that led to an attic floor with three small rooms that used to house up to six to eight servants. There was a closet with a port-a-potty in it and a small sink that was supposed to service those on the floor.

The two foster boys, Randy and Chris, slept in one room, the two younger foster girls, Abby and Sarah, slept in another room, and Libby had her own tiny space. The beds were no more than cots with one pillow and blanket. Each room had a small chest for their clothing. Libby had a mirror on her wall and a makeshift desk beneath it, on which she could do her homework.

The bedrooms on the second floor were much larger. The younger Thompson children shared bedrooms, with two children in each one, and their eldest child, Caleb, had his own room. The rooms each had antique bedroom furniture, including a queen bed, a chest of drawers with a mirror, a bench seat at the foot of the bed, and a small desk, all of it probably handed down through the generations of Thompsons before them. There was one large bathroom at the end of the hall to service all the children. If Libby wanted to shower, she had to do so before bed or in the wee hours of the morning to allow the Thompson children time to groom.

The main floor consisted of a large sitting room, a living room, a kitchen with a pantry, and a master bedroom suite. Mrs. Thompson did her best to keep the home clean, but the dust and cobwebs overtook most of the rooms.

For generations, the Thompsons had farmed the land and grew a variety of crops. They also raised cattle, pigs, and chickens. The pigpen housed up to ten hogs. They also had two chicken coops with approximately twenty hens and two roosters. There was a large barn where they stored their produce and one smaller building for curing meat. Out back was a large well with a bucket. In the kitchen sink was an old-fashioned pump that ran from the well. The workload on the farm was difficult, so when Mrs. Thompson suggested fostering older children as supplemental workers, Mr. Thompson agreed. They would be getting additional help on the farm and a monthly check to boot. They expected all the children to work hard, doing their fair share to justify having food, clothing, and a roof over their heads. The Thompsons spent little of the money received from the state on the children's needs. Instead, used it to purchase additional land and equipment to expand the farm. Libby suspected that the only reason the family took foster children into their home was to have free labor, but she never spoke up when the social worker came around for home visits for fear of retaliation. If she had learned nothing else from her prior experience in the foster system, it was to stay under the radar and out of the reach of prying eyes and angry fists.

Up at 4:30 a.m. every morning, Libby had to feed the chickens and slop the hogs before getting ready for school. It was hard enough for her, so she knew the younger children were struggling. If they failed to complete the chores, they knew what would be waiting. Mr. Thompson would sit on the front stoop, belt in hand, waiting for anyone who didn't complete their assigned chores. Out of empathy, Libby would hurry through her work and then backtrack to help the younger children.

Many days she had to rush just to catch the bus and thus was unable to clean the hog and chicken manure off her shoes, leaving a lingering odor. The kids on the bus were cruel and called the foster children names, such as foster pigs or orphan hogs. Libby was unsure why she let their words affect her so much, but she never allowed them to see how much their comments hurt her. She would gather up the younger children and walk past the others toward the back of the bus, far away from the other kids' jeers and snide remarks.

Libby wasn't sure if she blamed them for her hurt feelings or identified with their comments. Although cruel, their words were also true. Libby only owned one pair of shoes and would likely not get another pair soon, so the first place she went to when the bus dropped them off at school was the restroom to clean her shoes before heading to homeroom. It was one thing to have the kids on the bus tease her; it would be another to have an entire class make fun of her.

The bus ride home was the best part of her day as well as the worst, as she would have to go straight to completing her chores and then help prepare the evening meal. Mrs. Thompson was a great cook, but she was very disorganized, running Libby here and there during meal prep. By the time everyone finished eating, the dishes were washed, and Libby had helped the younger kids get ready for bed, and she finally sat down at her makeshift desk, she could hardly keep her eyelids open, so her grades began to drop. Her dream of being on the honor roll and getting a college scholarship was slipping. When the exhaustion was at its worst, she thought that taking the easy way out as Mr. Pike had done wasn't such a bad idea after all. If it weren't for the empathy that she felt for the younger children, she might have done something drastic.

Ms. McPherson was Libby's English teacher. Early on, she spotted that Libby had a real talent for writing. She had a grasp on the use of language that many of her counterparts didn't have at such a young age. Ms. McPherson looked forward to reading Libby's papers, and Libby received high marks for them. Ms. McPherson was certain that Libby would qualify to join the school paper staff and possibly win the writing contest and collect a $1,000 scholarship.

When Libby began falling asleep at her desk, and her grades began to drop, Ms. McPherson's concern peaked, as such behavior was so out of character for this bright young girl. Being careful not to draw attention to herself, Ms. McPherson began watching Libby closely, documenting any unusual behaviors. As Libby's conduct continued to worsen, she felt that it was time for a parent-teacher conference to find out what was going on. She sent letters to all the parents so as not to single Libby out and draw suspicion to her real motive, but she had decided that it was time to get to the bottom of the problem. Libby's future was bright, and the thought of someone or something altering her trajectory to academic success was not a light matter to Ms. McPherson.

The Thompsons showed up at the school prepared to meet, greet, and then leave the parent-teacher conference as soon as possible. Mr. Thompson felt like school was a waste of time. Being a successful school dropout himself, he thought that he was grooming his children to be prosperous regardless of their education, so it was no surprise that three of his five children had been held back a grade. What surprised Ms. McPherson is that no one had ever questioned his children's demeanor in the past or drawn attention to the obvious neglect of their educational needs.

To attend the parent-teacher conference, the Thompsons had left the other children in the care of their oldest, fifteen-year-old Caleb.

Caleb was trying his best to emulate his father. Mr. Thompson worked the children hard, believing he was developing their character. He rarely allowed them to rest and would not give them food or drink until the chores were completed. This was how Mr. Thompson's father had raised him, and if it was good enough for Mr. Thompson, it was good enough for them. Before leaving for the parent-teacher conference, Mr. Thompson challenged Caleb to keep the children busy, picking and husking the corn by hand, which Caleb vowed he would do. If there was one thing that Caleb valued, it was a word of praise from his father, which didn't come often or easily.

It was a hot afternoon, unusually tepid for that time of year. The temperature was holding around ninety-seven degrees, and the sun was beating down relentlessly. Caleb sent the children out to the field and demanded that they pick all the corn on the northwest corner of the field approximately a half mile from the house. Caleb was often tasked with looking after the younger children and was often blamed, criticized, and punished when they didn't perform to expectation. Caleb didn't want to show any sign of weakness by crying, so he would usually retaliate by belittling the younger ones as his father had done to him. It was a perpetual family behavior, passed down from father to son.

The children, already hot and sweaty, were exhausted from earlier chores. They knew that if they didn't comply, trouble would await them when Mr. Thompson returned, so rather than argue with Caleb, they trudged out into the field. He swore he would not allow them to drink until they picked and husked at least two bushels of corn. Caleb was not quite old enough to understand what dehydration was and how dangerous it could be, especially in children. He felt that he was obeying his father's rules and coveted the praise he would receive when his dad returned home. Caleb wanted to prove that he was old enough to run the farm.

Chris, who was nine years old, picked corn alongside twelve-year-old Randy. Chris hung out with Randy because he looked up to him, and Randy tried to keep Chris out of Mr. Thompson's way. Chris was a lovable kid but somewhat clumsy and slow, typical for his age, but Mr. Thompson was not having any of his shenanigans. The last time Chris didn't get his chores done on time, Mr. Thompson had locked him in the chicken coop until dusk and made him go to bed without supper. The other children cringed as they heard Chris wailing and begging to be released from the coop.

At bedtime, Chris curled up next to Randy in bed, his tummy growling, and cried himself to sleep. It broke Randy's heart and made him mad at himself that he had eaten his entire supper rather than sneak some of it up to the room for Chris. So, after the lights were out, and everyone was in bed, Randy slipped down the staircase to the kitchen to steal a biscuit for Chris. As he reached the bottom of the stairs, he accidentally kicked a boot off the step. It landed with a thud. As he stood in silence, he heard a door open. Moments later, the kitchen light turned on. Randy barely had time to slip into the pantry.

Through the crack in the door, he saw Mr. Thompson with his belt in hand, ready to beat the child who had dared to get out of bed after lights out. Mr. Thompson looked around the kitchen. When he was satisfied that no one was up, he grabbed the last biscuit off the plate and headed back to his room. Randy was devastated that the biscuit, which had been within his reach, was now gone. What would he give to Chris to silence his rumbling belly?

Looking around the pantry, he found a small package of cheese crackers that had fallen behind a bag of flour. *This will have to do,* he thought. He gently opened the pantry door and then crept back up the staircase to his room. Chris devoured the crackers while Randy prayed that no one would miss them. Randy promised himself that he would watch over Chris, and if he got into trouble again, Randy would be sure to save a portion of his meal for him, as it was far too dangerous to steal from the kitchen.

Thirty minutes into their work in the field, Chris began to complain of being thirsty. He told Randy that he was going to go get some water. Randy was certain that Caleb would not give him any, but he let Chris run back to the house to ask anyway. Just as Randy had supposed, Caleb would not give Chris any water. He merely reminded him of the rules and then sent him back out to the field.

The sun was high and hot, beating down on the children. Chris walked slowly back to Randy, but within five minutes was complaining again, only this time he said he was feeling dizzy, weak, and nauseous. Randy told him to sit under the shade of a large corn stalk. He ran back to the house to ask Caleb for some water. Randy figured that since he was older, Caleb would be less likely to say no.

Shortly after Randy left, Chris had a seizure, jerking around on the ground with no one around to help him. Each seizure lasted longer and longer until he quit breathing.

Randy arrived at the house and asked Caleb for a glass of water, but once again, he refused, telling Randy that until the work was complete, there would be no water breaks. Randy said he was worried about Chris, but all Caleb could think of was how proud his dad would be when he got home and saw the corn husked and ready for freezing.

By the time Randy got back to Chris, he was lying on the ground, motionless. When Randy reached down to help him up, Chris's skin felt hot and dry. His appearance scared Randy, so he shook him hard but could not rouse him. Randy ran back to the house as fast as his shaking legs would carry him, his heart pounding harder with each step while the ache in his heart grew because he knew Chris was in a bad way.

As soon as Randy saw Caleb in the distance, he began screaming that something was terribly wrong with Chris. Looking frustrated, Caleb told Randy that he was sure that Chris was merely faking it to get a drink. It took about five minutes of arguing with Caleb before Randy could convince him that Chris was not faking anything but that something was very wrong with him. Caleb was upset with Randy and told him that if Chris was faking it, they would both be in for a whooping when his dad got home.

By the time they made it back to Chris, his skin was red and translucent. Caleb bent down to grab his arm, so he could pick him up, but Chris's arm was limp and dropped back to the ground haphazardly.

"He's not faking, Caleb!" Randy cried. "Something is really wrong with him!"

Shaken, Caleb handed Randy his cell phone and told him to call 911. Caleb dropped the cup of water that he had been carrying and ran back to the house to call his father on the landline to assure him that the situation was not his fault. Caleb was correct in that it was actually his father's fault for leaving him in charge of enforcing rigid rules while knowing that Caleb was not old enough to understand when those rules needed to be broken. The only thing that had been broken that day was Chris's life, Randy's hope, and Caleb's future.

Meanwhile, at the school, Ms. McPherson sent Libby to the cafeteria for a cola while she spoke with the Thompsons. She began by telling them what a wonderful student Libby was but that she had begun to falter in her studies and would fall asleep at her desk. Mr. Thompson assured Ms. McPherson that they would tend to Libby, and she would do better from now on.

Ms. McPherson asked about Libby's daily routine at home in a way that made the Thompsons uncomfortable. Initially, Mrs. Thompson answered her questions, but as she began to get more specific and detailed with her inquiries, Mr. Thompson became defensive and obstinate and said he had had enough of her stupid questions and that it was none of her business anyway.

Caught off guard by his sudden outburst, Ms. McPherson tried to explain her concerns, which only made Mr. Thompson madder, and he cut her off, using filthy language. She looked at Mrs. Thompson, who was cowering in her chair. Ms. McPherson had seen that look before in battered women at the shelter where she volunteered and knew where the situation was going.

As the conversation grew louder, they heard ambulance sirens go past the school, heading in the direction of the farm. As Mr. Thompson continued to rant, Mrs. Thompson stood to look out the window. Within minutes of the sirens passing, Mr. Thompson's cell phone rang. Caleb was on the other end of the phone, crying and yelling that it was not his fault. With another outburst of filthy language, this time directed at Caleb, Mr. Thompson hung up, sneering at Ms. McPherson. "You keep your nose on your own face if you know what's good for you." With that he grabbed his wife and ran out the door. When Mrs. Thompson asked Mr. Thompson about the call, Ms. McPherson overheard his response. "You stupid woman. Just shut your mouth and do as I tell you." Ms. McPherson was left dazed and confused at her desk, wondering what had just happened.

Mr. and Mrs. Thompson not only left the school without explanation, they also left without Libby. When Libby sauntered into the classroom, Ms. McPherson was surprised to see she was still there.

"Where are the Thompsons?" Libby asked. With a look of concern on her face, Ms. McPherson replied that they had received a call from Caleb and then left without an explanation. She offered to give Libby a ride home if she could wait for Ms. McPherson to complete her last bit of paperwork. Libby agreed and sat in the hall, sipping her cola and wondering what would cause the Thompsons to leave in such a hurry, forgetting about her. Perhaps they had done it on purpose and expected her to walk home, after which they would chide her for not getting her chores done on time. Although she was curious, she enjoyed having a bit of time to sit in the cool air rather than work out in the heat. She would pay the piper later, but for the moment, she was going to sit back, relax, and enjoy her cola because she didn't know when she would have another one. The Thompsons didn't purchase such luxuries for the foster kids, yet they and their own children enjoyed one with each supper meal while the rest of the children drank unfiltered well water.

Ms. McPherson finished her paperwork and stuck her head out into the hall to tell Libby that it was time to go. Her voice pulled Libby out of her slumber. "Back to the grind," Libby muttered under her breath, not wanting Ms. McPherson to hear. She knew that she was already in enough hot water.

They arrived at the farm just as the ambulance was leaving. They saw Mr. and Mrs. Thompson standing on the front porch talking with a police officer. Caleb was sitting in the swing, staring out into the field. It was obvious that he had been crying because his face was red and his eyes were still moist with tears.

Ms. McPherson turned to Libby. "You stay close to the car, and I'll go find out what's going on." As Libby exited the car, Randy ran up to her and told her that something had happened to Chris and that he was afraid that Chris was going to die.

Seeing Randy run to the car, Ms. McPherson hurried around to Libby's side, then stooped down to look Randy in the eye and ask what had happened. After reciting the events to Ms. McPherson, Randy began to sob. "I tried to help him," he cried, "but Caleb wouldn't listen to me. By the time we got back to the field with water, Chris looked funny and wasn't moving. Caleb got scared and made me call 911 while he went back to the house to call his dad." Ms. McPherson felt a chill climb up her spine but tried to remain composed for the children.

Libby was old enough to understand the severity of the situation. She cried silently, tears rolling down her cheeks as she thought about poor Chris. He was such a sweet little boy, always smiling and laughing. He didn't deserve this; no child did. She could feel the anger building inside of her next to the hopelessness she felt, knowing there was nothing that she could do. What would happen now?

Ms. McPherson embraced both children until the police officer came over to speak with Randy. After Randy relayed his version of the story, and Ms. McPherson informed the officer that they were foster children, it was obvious to the officer that he needed to contact social services about the other children. He walked back to his cruiser, picked up his radio, and called for social services to come to the farm. Dispatch sent his message forward with a "stat" notation attached.

The notification came later that evening that they were unable to resuscitate Chris. His time of death was recorded as 6:43 p.m. Within minutes of the call from the hospital, the social worker was at the door of the farmhouse, and all of the remaining foster children were removed from the home with a warning to the Thompsons that she would be back to discuss the treatment of their own biological children as well.

Mr. Thompson was no longer spewing his hateful, filthy language. Instead, he wondered if the police would take him away in handcuffs as he remembered his daddy being taken away in handcuffs when he was a child. Rather than learn from his father's mistakes he had repeated them.

Mrs. Thompson simply went into the house to prepare supper as if nothing had happened. It was not the first time the police had been to her home, and nothing had ever changed before. There was no reason for her to believe that she would not receive another beating from her husband if supper was not on the table by 7:00 sharp. She barely had enough time, so she could not waste a minute checking on her children. They would have to fend for themselves.

Libby and the other foster children went to a local shelter for the night. It started to feel like a horrible nightmare to her. As the oldest foster child, she needed to hold it together, so the other children would not be scared. She had done her best to protect the children and was beginning to feel a pang of guilt for not being there for Chris. She had already let Adam down. The weight of responsibility was far too heavy for Libby to bear.

When they arrived at the shelter, a warm supper was waiting for them. It had been a while since any of the children had eaten enough to keep their bellies from rumbling at bedtime, as the Thompson's had rationed each meal to the bare minimum. At the table sat a young boy named Isaac, who quickly hit it off with Randy. Shortly after the meal, the children brushed their teeth, changed into their pajamas, and were ushered into a small ward with six beds. Unlike the warmth of the dining hall, the room was void of any decoration or color, but each child would have their own bed to sleep in, as only one bed was occupied by Isaac.

Thinking of Chris, Randy asked Libby if she felt it would be OK if he slept with Isaac, who readily agreed to let him do so. Abby and Sarah slipped into bed with Libby, sheepish looks on their faces. Libby looked at their small frames and sunken eyes and nodded approvingly, then rolled over to snuggle with them.

The social worker checked on the children an hour later, only to find just two of the beds occupied. Her heart ached as she wondered what the children had endured and how much counseling it might take for them to recuperate from the horrors of living with the Thompsons. The system had failed these children, and she vowed she would not let such an atrocity happen again. She bent down to kiss each one goodnight and tuck in their covers.

When she reached Libby, the girl's eyelids fluttered open. She looked deep into the eyes of the social worker as if questioning her intent. "I know you tried your best to care for these children, Libby," the social worker said, "and I'm so sorry I didn't do a better job of helping you. I promise I'll find them loving, caring homes." With that promise, Libby was finally able to close her eyes and fall into a deep and much-needed sleep.

Over the next few weeks, the social worker came through on her promise to Libby and handpicked a home for each of the children. She chose only homes that had a proven track record of being loving and caring, just as she had told Libby that she would do. Libby asked to leave the shelter last, so she could participate in each child's placement interview. It was helpful and healing for Libby to meet those families and "hand off" each child with a kiss goodbye and a promise to see them soon. Libby didn't enjoy staying in the shelter for so long, but she felt it was her duty to ensure that the younger children had proper homes with loving caregivers.

When she believed her goal was accomplished, she informed the social worker that she was ready to be placed herself, so the process of finding Libby a home began. After going through four family placement interviews, they settled on the Nelsons.

CHAPTER
FIVE

Before arriving at Mr. and Mrs. Nelson's home, Libby had been through three temporary foster homes. By then she was becoming a very beautiful young woman. At 5 foot, 7 inches and 115 pounds, she was well developed with a petite frame and long brunette hair. Her facial features were soft with bright blue eyes and long lashes, and one look from her could melt away any resistance. Her gait was smooth, using long strides with a posture that revealed an inner strength and confidence. She was beginning to cause the heads of more than a few young men to turn as she walked by. At seventeen years old, she was one month into her junior year of high school.

The Nelsons were a middle-aged couple with two grown children who were married and out of the home and a late-in-life eighteen-year-old son named James. Their home was in a middle-to upper-class neighborhood and was picture perfect in appearance. The lawn was beautifully manicured. Libby's first impression of the home's appearance brought back memories of her own home long ago. How Libby missed that house and her parents.

The Nelsons' house was a two-story cape cod with a wrap-around porch. The windows had black shutters and flower boxes overflowing with beautiful arrangements. The right side of the porch held a swing that was scattered with cushions and pillows, inviting someone to sit and chew the fat. On the left side of the porch sat two rockers with a small table between to hold drinks while people sat and discussed the latest news in town. Both sides of the house had French doors. The front door was large with two side windows. The entire front of the home was nearly all windows, which let in a ton of sunlight.

Mrs. Nelson was an impeccable housekeeper and an even better cook. There was little for Libby to complain about, although she had no real expectations. She was struggling to maintain hope but kept telling herself that she only needed to make it through her senior year, and she would be able to move out on her own. She had been dreaming for years of being on her own. She imagined moving into a small apartment with a dog and finding a job close enough to walk or ride a bike back and forth. Meanwhile, Libby kept her guard up, as she had been through too many abusive foster homes to let it down. At that point she felt that she could not experience anything worse than what she had already, or could she?

James had his own room, as did Libby. His room was a large attic space with hard-rock and football posters decorating the walls. A king-size bed stood in the corner of the room, which still left enough space for an air-hockey table, a pool table, and a basketball shooting machine. He had a stereo hooked up to surround sound, his own sixty-five-inch television with a video game system and a laptop. Libby could not imagine such extravagance lavished on one child. On his door was a large sign that said, "Do Not Enter," as if she would ever want to enter his room for any reason. James liked to flaunt his advantages over Libby, making it hard for her to want to like him enough to get to know him better. She just kept her distance, acting cordial and civil but also cool and detached. She would take special care to note where James was when he was home, so she could avoid running into him, especially when his parents were out. Every time he looked at her, she felt uncomfortable, even though he was disarming and attractive. She knew boys like James were a danger to girls like her.

James was the quarterback of the high school football team and all-time favorite to win most valuable player along with a full-ride scholarship to an Ivy League college. He was around six feet tall, dark skinned, and muscular. He had chiseled features, and when he flashed his pearly white smile, dimples grew on either side of his face. His brown hair lay in waves on his head, and his blue eyes sparkled when he laughed or, worse, when he was up to something. The girls flocked around him, willing to do anything for his attention, which was sickening to Libby. She felt he was arrogant, condescending, and spoiled, but she was not going to make waves. She just wanted to survive the remainder of high school and then make her own life. If that meant putting up with a little attitude from James in the meantime, so be it. She had decided she was not about to be a victim again. If she had to stand up to James, she would, but she preferred to stay out of his way, out of his sight, and certainly out of his mind.

The Nelsons were decent enough people. Both were retired, but Mr. Nelson continued to do some consulting for a large retail company, and Mrs. Nelson helped a local accountant during tax season. Their only real flaw was in believing that James could do no wrong. When he came home and produced a fake report card that put him on the honor roll, they bought him a black jeep with all the bells and whistles. When he won the homecoming game and was announced as homecoming king, they gave him permission to go on a weekend camping trip with his friends. Of course, he swore that no girls would be there, when in reality, the trip would be a drunken coed party. Libby was well aware of his antics but never breathed a word of them to anyone, least of all the Nelsons. She vowed to simply mind her own business and focus on her grades and her future independence.

Libby's talent as a journalist continued to blossom. By mid-year she was voted as the new editor of the school paper, which garnered her an after-school job at the local town paper as a "go-fer." She was gaining experience with editing and typesetting as well as shadowing the reporters. The job didn't pay well, but the experience was well worth the effort, and she was able to save a little for college and an occasional trip to the mall.

One week she was able to purchase a new top and a nice pair of jeans. Libby was not pretentious, but the store was having a huge sale, and she saved over 50 percent with a coupon she had found online. At last she began to feel some hope again. Soon she would be off to college and on her own. Libby had dreamed of that day ever since she was old enough to work small jobs at her parents' store. She had hoped to take over the business when her parents retired. Even at the young age of ten, she was able to call in orders, stock shelves, and use the cash register. At times she even helped her mother with the books. Thinking of the store brought back bittersweet memories of her parents. Some days Libby missed them so much that she felt an ache in her chest. When she focused, she swore she could even smell the scent of her father's aftershave and her mother's perfume. She drank in those memories like a thirsting deer.

The weekend of the big camping trip arrived. James had his camping gear packed and placed in the jeep and then headed next door to see his neighbor. Keith had lived next door to the Nelsons for the past eight years. He was a creepy sort of fellow with long, stringy hair and a gothic look who wore black most of the time. Libby's bedroom window faced his bedroom, and many nights she would hear him blaring his hard-rock music. He had never done anything for Libby to dislike him, but she made sure to stay out of his path as well. Ever since Keith had turned twenty-one, he had supplied James with alcohol almost every weekend. James would give him an extra twenty dollars each time Keith bought beer or wine for him, so it was a lucrative venture that he intended to continue. That weekend Keith had purchased four cases of beer for James. As James reached for his wallet to pay Keith, he realized he had left it in the bathroom while he was getting ready. Promising to return, James headed back to the house to retrieve his wallet, so he could get the weekend party started.

Meanwhile, Libby was headed to the shower. She had the opportunity to shadow a reporter who was doing a story on teenage drinking in small-town America. She turned on the shower and had begun to undress when James burst into the room. She grabbed a towel to wrap around her but not before James got a good look, which caused a smile, or, rather, a smirk to spread across his face. Libby demanded that he leave, but he just looked at her and laughed, telling her that he had no interest in her when he had his pick of the cheerleaders.

He's such a jerk, she thought.

He grabbed his wallet off the vanity and turned to leave but not before yanking the towel away from Libby. She screamed and pushed him out the door so hard that he fell into the hallway. Red-faced, she slammed the door, making sure to lock it behind him. She heard him laughing as he bolted down the stairs. She was so angry that all she could do was stand there and cry.

Soon, she heard his jeep drive away. She was thankful that he was gone for the weekend because she was not sure that she could stomach seeing him anytime soon. She continued with her shower, which washed her tears down the drain, the noise of the falling water covering the sound of her crying. It made her angry that she had allowed James to cause her to cry. She took a deep breath and swore he would never get the best of her again.

At 7:00 that evening, she met up with Olivia, a twenty-three-year-old budding journalist. With her was eighteen-year-old Brian, her part-time camera operator. Olivia was tall and thin with jet-black shoulder-length hair, a beautiful smile, and a contagious laugh. She was fun to be around but took her job very seriously. Her dark eyes were piercing, so being on the other end of her interview was somewhat intimidating. Olivia had a knack for getting her story. That night they were headed to a local campground well known for teenage drinking parties. Her goal was to catch the story of her young career and reap the top award offered to her small local paper. Reporters dreamed about putting their byline on the next big breaking news story, which was a gateway to more prestigious jobs in the city. Libby felt honored that Olivia had chosen her to be part of this adventure and was determined to make her proud by doing her best.

Brian and Libby began loading the equipment into the van. Brian was about five foot ten and stocky, built like a bodybuilder. Libby found out later that he was a senior at her high school and a nose guard on the football team. Hearing that he was a football player caused Libby's hackles to rise, but he was so kind and respectful, with a meek and gentle manner about him, that she let her guard down a little with him. He knew James and didn't like him at all. He described James much as Libby had, only Brian added "rude and disrespectful to girls" to the list. Brian could not understand why the girls flocked around James when he treated them so badly. James had a habit of taking advantage of girls and then blabbing it to the entire football team. When James started his lewd stories, and his teammates hunkered around James for the sordid details, Brian would leave the room. It made Brian angry. His sentiment toward James earned him a soft spot in Libby's heart.

Instantly becoming friends, Brian and Libby chatted the entire way to the campground, which was about thirty minutes outside of town in a wooded area known as Muscle Creek. It received its name because local jocks were known for having their wild weekend parties there. Rumor had it that high school football teams would invite girls there and then drug their drinks and take advantage of them. None of the girls had ever come forward out of fear and shame, so the football players generally got away with their illegal capers.

Libby's high school team, which was favored to win the state championship, something they had not done in over twenty years, was scheduled to play the following weekend, so they planned to party it up this weekend. Because the teachers, coaches, and parents didn't want any of the players suspended from the team, they overlooked any indiscretions that the boys were rumored to have committed. Besides, they convinced themselves that if the boys had done anything illegal, surely someone would have come forward already. It seemed the whole town had ignored the rumors, and Olivia was determined to put a stop to it with her written campground documentary.

The van arrived at the campground at around dusk. They could see campfires glowing as the sound of music and laughter grew louder. They slipped into the woods so as not to arouse suspicion. Olivia went to the left, Brian went to the right, and Libby went down the middle. The first one to run across some action was to notify the other two. Each had a cell phone with snap chat tracking engaged. They were to text if they saw anything suspicious to maintain silence. Using snap chat, the others would track their location. Libby was somewhat nervous but also excited to help Olivia catch her first big scoop.

Libby slipped through the trees as stealthily as she could. She had not gone a hundred yards when she stopped short, hearing moaning and heavy breathing. She crouched down and crept forward. As her eyes adjusted to the darkness, she saw James with one of the cheerleaders, a pretty girl named Lisa. Her long blonde hair was braided and pinned up on her head in a bun. She was wearing tight skinny jeans and a revealing halter-top. Libby could not help but notice that most of the cheerleaders dressed provocatively. Lisa and James were making out hot and heavy, which made Libby want to hurl. If she had had any regard for James at all, she lost it at that moment.

When James stopped necking to pour another drink for Lisa, Libby saw him slip something into the drink. Lisa's speech was already slurred, and as she stood to walk, she stumbled. Before she could take the drink from James, she floundered and hit the ground. James became irate and began to belittle her, calling her names like "sleaze bag" and "trailer trash." He grabbed her arms and yanked her to her feet, then started to pour the drink down her throat. Lisa choked and recoiled, turning away from him, which only fueled his anger. He shoved her against a tree and yelled at her, continuing to call her names. He said she was a pathetic cheerleader and that he wouldn't be caught dead in public with her. He said the reason he brought her out into the woods was that he didn't want anyone to see him with her. As Lisa began to cry, he slapped her face and ordered her to get out of his sight. She continued to cry as she ran away, stumbling through the brush, nearly hitting Libby yet not noticing her there.

Libby was disgusted at James behavior, especially considering the earlier incident in the bathroom. She was so angry that she forgot to radio Olivia and Brian as planned and instead stepped out into the clearing to confront him.

"You think you're all that!" Libby yelled. Caught off guard, James turned toward her. "I saw you spike her drink," she continued, her rage growing. "Were you planning to drug her, so you could take advantage of her? Well, it looks like your little fishing episode has failed since your fish got away. You won't have any big fish stories to tell your team tomorrow."

Instead of becoming furious, James took a step back and gave Libby a once-over that immediately caused her to blush. He walked around Libby, eyeing her up and down. "I don't think that my fish got away," he sneered. "I think my real catch is you."

He grabbed Libby and forced her to the ground. His breath was vile, and his hands were all over her. Before she could object, he was on top of her. She struggled beneath his weight as he pinned her to the ground. Libby could only imagine the worst.

Was he really going to do this to her? Without help, the dreams she had for her future would not become a reality.

Before she could utter a sound or cry for help, something flew out the tree line and slammed into James, knocking him several feet away from Libby. As soon as his weight lifted, she rolled the opposite way, got to her feet, and ran straight back to the van as quickly as her wobbly legs would carry her. Her new top was torn, and the zipper on her jeans was broken. By the time she reached the van, she was in tears. Had her foster brother James really attempted to rape her? She jumped into the van, locked the door, and buried her head in her hands. She didn't raise her head again until she heard Brian's voice.

"Libs, are you OK?"

Unbeknownst to Libby, Brian had heard her yelling at James and ran to help her. When he arrived at the clearing and saw James on top of her, he went into a frenzy. Brian never saw Libby get up and run because he was too focused on beating James. When he was done with James, the quarterback was nothing but a pile of whimpering flesh. Brian radioed Olivia, who called the police. Within minutes, several squad cars had the camp surrounded and gathered up as many teens as they could catch. Several of the girls were unconscious and partially dressed.

Brian handed over a stash of pills to the police that had fallen from James's pocket when he sent him flying. After taking blood tests on the girls and analyzing the pills, the lab tech reported that each girl had Rohypnol in her system, a date-rape drug. It seemed that this time the football team was not going to get away with their scheme. Libby was thrilled that James would have to pay the piper but apprehensive about what it would mean for her living with the Nelsons, as she knew that she would have to testify to what she had seen James do to the cheerleader and what he had attempted to do to her. Her mind was in a fog, her future was treacherously unclear.

Olivia finally achieved her first big byline. The story was front-page news "Local Football Team Accused of Drugging Young Women." Several teens were arrested, many of them star football players. With pressure from the press, the school had no choice but to suspend the players. James and two other boys were removed from the football team when it was reported that they bore the brunt of responsibility for drugging some of the girls. The players had been spiking drinks and molesting girls for several weeks.

Once the story hit the news, girls came forward in droves to file charges. James's illustrious career as the star quarterback and all-American boy was crashing down around him. His parents felt that, under the circumstances, it was in their best interest that Libby leave their home with no apologies and no amends.

As soon as the news hit the front page, people began treating Libby like a pariah. The Nelsons refused to believe that their son could do such a thing. When girl after girl came forward with new evidence, however, the news made national headlines: "Star football stand-out accused of drugging and raping numerous girls." Eventually, their disbelief gave way to the revelation that their son was not who they thought, and the Nelsons began family counseling as they awaited trial. Libby's testimony was not needed in court due to the nine other depositions that the district attorney had accumulated against James. It appeared that he would have to kiss his football scholarship goodbye and that he was facing the real possibility of some hard time for his indiscretions. His life was ruined. He hated Libby and blamed her for his misfortunes, never accepting culpability. He vowed that she would pay for ruining his life. He warned that she had best keep looking over her shoulder from now on because he would find her no matter where she went, and she would be sorry. The thought of Matt, and now James, finishing what they started to do to Libby reverberated in her mind, causing her to build an even bigger wall around her life.

CHAPTER
SIX

Since Libby was seventeen and nearing legal age, temporary foster homes seemed the best solution. Every couple of months she moved to a new home as families took on younger children to replace her.

Her last home was with the Hydes. Mr. Hyde and his wife were partners in business and in life. They owned a large plant nursery with an adjoining flower shop. The nursery sat on a plot of land that was approximately eleven acres, where most of their plants were grown. Little of their stock for sale was ordered in; most of it was locally grown. Since Mrs. Hyde was never able to have children, they had worked hard at developing a flourishing business and serving their community.

The Hydes were a church-going couple who spent much of their free time involved in ministry activities. They particularly loved helping with the kids' club and vacation Bible school. Working with the children filled a void in their lives and took some of the sting out of not being able to have their own children.

Mr. Hyde was an elder in the church and a strong mentor to younger men. He had a degree in biblical counseling that came in handy when young couples had marital spats or younger men were struggling to keep their minds pure amongst the many temptations that were readily available all around. He also took turns teaching the adult Sunday school class.

Mrs. Hyde led the women's group, which oversaw hospitality events and outreach ministry to young mothers and widows. She met Mr. Hyde while they were attending Grace Bible College. They were in a course together on marital counseling. One day after class, Mr. Hyde had literally bumped into Mrs. Hyde, causing her to drop her books and sending her notes flying everywhere. As they bent down to gather everything up, their eyes locked. Mr. Hyde said he knew right then that she was the one that the Lord had chosen for him. He asked her out for coffee to apologize for his clumsiness and then invited her to church with him the following Sunday. Two years later, they had both graduated and planned their wedding shortly after.

The Hydes reminded Libby so much of her parents that she immediately felt a kinship with them. They felt the same way about her, and before long, it felt as if Libby had always been part of their lives. She bore such a striking resemblance to Mrs. Hyde that when they met people out on the street, folks naturally assumed that Libby was the Hydes' daughter.

They had decided not to push Libby into attending church until she felt ready, as Libby still struggled with God allowing her parents to die and for her experiences in the foster system. If God loved her, why had He let so many bad things happen?

It didn't take long before the Hydes realized that they could trust Libby, so they offered her a job at their business. She jumped at the opportunity to earn some cash. Since Libby's social life was virtually nonexistent, most, if not all, of her earnings would go into her college fund. Mr. Hyde also began teaching Libby about investing money. Finally, after many years in foster care, Libby had found a home with a couple whom she felt she could call family. The Hydes felt much the same way toward Libby.

In time they trusted her enough to run the business. It had been years since the Hydes had taken a vacation, and with Libby doing a bang-up job at the shop, they began to plan the vacation of a lifetime. They were going to go on a three-month tour of Germany, Switzerland, and Great Britain. Libby felt honored that they were going to entrust her with their livelihood and vowed to make them proud.

As her eighteenth birthday and graduation approached, Libby began sending off college applications. She met with her school counselor, Clara Rust. Clara was a middle-aged woman with an engaging smile and a personality to match. She was instrumental in Libby's success, as she had encouraged her to take dual-degree courses that would count as credit toward her college degree. Libby already had enough credits to count for a full semester of college. Clara had also helped Libby devote time to pursuing journalism. This came in handy as Libby began journaling to help her deal with the memories that would plague her while she slept. After meeting with the school counselor, she felt confident that she could get at least an interview with one of the Ivy League colleges where she had submitted applications.

The Hydes were due to return from their tour in August, so Libby would have plenty of time to prepare for her move to college. She began to mentally pack what she would need for her dorm room. She found a cute bed set at a department store with sheets and curtains to match. The Hydes said she could take the scanner/printer from the guest room with her so she would not have to run to the library to print her assignments. Unsure if she would have her own bathroom or a community washroom, she didn't take the time to look at bathroom rugs, but she did order a set of towels and washcloths. She also made a list of toiletries and essentials that she would need such as a blow dryer, curling iron, microwave, coffee pot, and a mini fridge.

The more she envisioned her move, the more excited she became, ready to start her college experience. She applied to Harvard, Columbia, and Rutgers. She had learned so much about business and investing from Mr. Hyde that she wanted to major in business management and minor in financial planning. Each of the universities had received special academic recognition for their outstanding programs in these degrees, so Libby felt certain that her life was finally on the right track. Her grades had improved so much that she was looking at being the valedictorian for her graduating class. She had shown her ability to overcome adversity in her life and felt that her college application essay would prove her tenacity and capability to succeed at whatever she chose to do. During the final weeks before graduation, she focused on keeping her grades high and learning to run the Hydes' business. Life was good.

The Hydes were scheduled to fly out for the first leg of their vacation the Monday after graduation. There were many activities for them to plan that kept them super busy, so busy that Libby didn't want to break their momentum by discussing her own excitement about graduation and college. She didn't want to distract them from planning their itinerary. Every night they would get on the computer and pull up different tourist destinations, eagerly discussing the type of currency used for that country and where the best tourist spots were. Instead of changing the subject to graduation, Libby dove into helping the Hydes tie up the loose ends of their travel arrangements. She was so happy that she could play a small role in helping them achieve this long-awaited adventure, but as graduation day approached, her own anticipation began to mount along with some anxiety at being alone for three months over the summer. She pushed that thought to the back of her mind for the moment.

The graduation ceremony was beautiful. As valedictorian, Libby gave the graduation send-off speech. "To my fellow students," she began, "Many of us have had to endure undue hardships, obstacles, and setbacks in our lives that were not easy to overcome. We have suffered losses and some humiliation, but each experience became a preparation for what was to come. As we move to the next stage of our lives, some of us will head off to college, others will start their work career, and some will get married and start a family. My admonition is to pursue whatever comes in your future with grit, grace, and gumption and with a mindset of being the best of who we are and who we will become."

Her words were poignant and inspirational, which garnered her a standing ovation. As she crossed the stage to accept her diploma, she felt that life could not get any better. She looked out over the sea of people who had just stood and praised this little orphan girl, and her heart swelled with pride and gratitude. Her only regret was that her parents were not there to see the success that she had become. Tears started to well up as she walked off the stage, but she held her head high, focusing on not tripping down the steps.

After congratulating her fellow classmates and friends, Libby and the Hydes headed home. It was a gorgeous day with the sun shining and a balmy breeze in the air. Libby sat in the backseat with the window down and her eyes closed, soaking up the sun rays and letting the breeze flow over her face.

As she let herself relax, her mind drifted to Brian. She had not seen him since she left the Nelsons. She wished she could have had a chance to get to know him better or at least stayed in touch with him.

Before she could daydream any further, the car pulled into the driveway. As she opened her eyes, she noted several cars lining the street. *Wow,* she thought. *Someone must be having a party.*

She exited the car and headed for the front door with the Hydes close behind, chattering and laughing about something funny that Mr. Hyde had said. They were so happy, they almost seemed giddy. Libby once again had a feeling of satisfaction knowing that she had a small part in helping them prepare for their dream vacation.

Upon entering the house, Libby saw a large manila envelope on the entrance table in the hallway. That was usually where the mail dropped, along with the car keys and cell phones. She noted that the large envelope was addressed to her, and the return address was Harvard. Her heart began to beat a little faster as she looked back at the Hydes, who were grinning from ear to ear.

"Go ahead and open it, dear," Mrs. Hyde said.

With trembling hands, Libby picked up the envelope and carefully opened the seal, then slowly pulled out the letter. "Congratulations" was the first word that Libby saw. Her heart began to race, almost beating out of her chest. She looked up at the Hydes, beaming with pride. "I did it!" Libby exclaimed. "I've been accepted to the Harvard School of Business!"

"Libby, you have two more letters sitting there for you," Mr. Hyde said. She looked at the table and saw two smaller envelopes, one from Columbia and the other from Rutgers. She ripped both of them open, and her eyes brimmed with tears. Libby, the little orphan girl who had been shipped from foster home to foster home, abused and rejected for almost eight years, had been accepted to three of the most prestigious colleges in the nation. She felt as if she were in a dream, afraid that she would wake up any moment. Mr. and Mrs. Hyde embraced Libby.

"You have some decisions to make over the next few weeks," Mr. Hyde said, "but for now I've prepared something for the grill, so let's head out to the backyard and enjoy some steak."

Mr. Hyde led the way to the backyard, followed by Mrs. Hyde and Libby, her head still in the clouds as she tried to wrap her mind around being accepted into three prestigious colleges.

The Hydes lived in an upscale neighborhood. The backyard was surrounded by a white vinyl privacy fence. The covered porch extended from one end of the house to the other with a large gazebo attached to one corner and the garage to the other. In the gazebo was an outside kitchen with a built-in grill, a large counter, and an under-counter fridge with room enough for a table and six chairs. To the left of the gazebo was a large swimming pool with a slide. There was an entrance to the house where a laundry room and half bath were located, so they could drop wet clothes before entering the home and use the restroom without traipsing water into the house. Lounge chairs surrounded the pool with scattered tables for drinks. The yard was large to accommodate many guests.

In her oblivion, Libby didn't notice the fifty or more people standing in the backyard until they yelled, "Surprise!" No longer able to contain her tears, Libby let them flow freely down her cheeks. Mrs. Hyde stepped forward to wipe them away, handing her a tissue.

"I don't know what to say," Libby cried. "This is far more than I ever expected. When did you have time to do all of this?" Mrs. Hyde just smiled as Mr. Hyde handed Libby a set of keys. "What's this?" Libby asked. At that point she was barely managing a whisper, as she could not catch her breath, her heart beating so quickly.

"Why don't we go and see?" Mr. Hyde replied.

He took Libby's hand and led her around the side of the house to the garage. Libby had wondered why they didn't pull their car into the garage as they normally did but figured that since the day was so nice, they were going to leave the car outside for a while. As Mr. Hyde opened the garage, Libby saw a brand-new bright red convertible mini coupe. She was beside herself. "Is this for me?" she asked.

"See if the key fits," Mr. Hyde said, laughing.

Libby ran her hand across the smooth metal of the car toward the door. As she opened the car door, the smell of new leather filled her nostrils. She took a deep breath, inhaling the smell of a sweet and generous new life.

As she turned to thank the Hydes, she was met by a surprise. Could he really be there? She rubbed her eyes, thinking they might be playing tricks on her since she entered a dark garage from the sunny outdoors. When she opened her eyes, however, he was still there.

"Brian, is that really you?" she asked.

Brian stepped forward and hugged Libby. "How are you doing, Libs?"

Libby stood back and looked at Brian as if to make sure she was not imagining him. "How did you get here?" she asked.

"Well, aren't you happy to see me?" Brian replied.

"Of course," she replied. "Very happy, just surprised."

"Well, this is a surprise party," Brian quipped.

Libby found out later that Brian had kept in contact with the Hydes after Libby's placement with them. He had met them at the trial for James while Brian was covering the story with Olivia. The social worker had asked the Hydes to be present at the trial to get a little background of what Libby's life had been like. She had been through a rather traumatic event, and the social worker wanted the Hydes to be sure that they felt they could handle the possible psychological fallout that Libby may experience. The Hydes were exceptional people and quickly assured the social worker that they knew in their hearts that God had sent Libby to them, and their home was open and ready to receive her whenever she was ready to come.

At the trial, Brian made his way to the social worker to inquire about Libby. That was when he met the Hydes. They hit it off right away. The Hydes had grown fond of Brian over the past year as they kept in constant contact, relaying Libby's successes to Brian. Mr. Hyde even met with his friend, the editor of the local paper, to secure a job for Brian if he wanted it. It was a great opportunity for Brian to advance his career in journalism, so Brian accepted it on the spot. Besides that, it would allow him the time and proximity to get to know Libby better, so accepting the job and relocating was a no-brainer. As he stood there, face to face with her, he knew he had made the right decision.

"You look great, Libs," Brian said with true admiration, "and it sounds like you have the brains to go along with all that beauty.

Valedictorian, huh?" Libby blushed at his words but was happy that Brian thought she was smart and beautiful. She wondered where this relationship could go.

Back at the party, Libby walked from person to person, thanking everyone for coming and for being a positive influence on her. She was having such a wonderful time. Her heart could barely contain all the blessings she received: graduation, valedictorian, college acceptance, a new car, and now the chance to find out if there was something special blooming between her and Brian. She felt good knowing that in the Hydes' absence, she would have Brian around for company.

As the party began to wind down, Libby took her gifts and cards into the house. With all the excitement of the day, she hadn't had time to open any of them. Once in the house, she felt exhausted and opted to wait until later to open them. She was not sure that she was emotionally stable enough to handle more blessings. She wanted to savor the day and, when opening her gifts, savor the memory of it, a memory that would be etched in her mind for the rest of her life.

Mrs. Hyde and Libby cleaned up inside while Mr. Hyde and Brian did the same outside. With the cleaning complete, Libby was ready for bed. She and Brian had made plans to take the Hydes to the airport on Monday, so she would have someone with her after she said goodbye to them. Knowing that Libby would not have to be alone after their plane departed made the Hydes feel much better as well.

As for Brian, he lifted a small prayer of thanks to God for allowing him the opportunity to advance his career and for a chance to get to explore a possible relationship with Libby, a girl who made his heart skip a beat every time she was near and who stayed on his mind far too much of the time.

CHAPTER
SEVEN

The Hydes gave Brian their emergency contact numbers and charged him with watching over Libby in their absence, a job he eagerly accepted. He was thankful to them for their faith and trust in him, taking their charge to watch out for Libby very seriously. The send-off at the airport was bittersweet as they all hugged and said their goodbyes. They waved back and forth until they could no longer see one another. Hand in hand, the Hydes disappeared into the terminal, headed for London.

Libby was not a bit embarrassed to bury her head in Brian's chest and cry. She felt comfortable letting her defenses down in front of Brian, which was unusual for her. Over her years in the foster-care system, she had built up a wall that kept most people out and shielded her from additional hurts, which she had grown to expect.

With Brian, things were different. She felt as if she could truly be herself around him and tell him anything, and he would still accept her and be her friend.

The ride home from the airport was quiet. Libby had asked Brian to drive, as she expected that she would not be in the frame of mind to do so after the Hydes departed. It was a beautiful day, so Brian put the top down on Libby's mini coupe, turned the radio to an easy listening station, and watched as Libby laid her head back on the headrest and fell asleep. It took about thirty minutes to get home, and Brian savored every moment that he got to glance at Libby and soak in her radiant beauty, which was enhanced by the sunshine reflecting off her tanned skin.

Once they were back at the house, Brian ordered a pizza, and they settled in to open Libby's cards and gifts. Brian was surprised that she could wait so long to open them. Libby said that she had already received so much on graduation day that she was not sure that her heart could take any more. Now that the Hydes were safely off the ground and on their way to London, she needed something to cheer her up. She opened one card after the other, all of them filled with well wishes and money, lots of money. Once again, Libby felt humbled at the outpouring of love she had received. After opening the sixth card, the doorbell rang.

"That will be the pizza," Brian said. "Keep opening your cards, and I'll be right back."

Libby heard Brian bantering with the delivery boy. He was so good with people, having a magnetic personality that put most folks at ease. She opened the next card, which was somewhat odd. It was not a graduation card but a "thinking of you" card. As she read the message, her heart dropped. "I have been thinking of you every day for the past few years," it said. "You were the one that got away, but NOT FOR LONG! I'll be seeing you soon." There was no signature. Libby felt an oppressive sensation of impending doom.

As Brian entered the room with the pizza, she tried to shake it off. With his keen reporter intuition, however, Brian sensed that something was wrong, and he pressed Libby to find out. He finally wore her down, and she handed the card to him. He noted immediately that there was no postmark on the envelope, meaning it had been hand delivered and not mailed. The realization sunk in that whoever had left it had been to Libby's home. This was not something she had considered, but now that she did, her mind was reeling, and an uneasy feeling set in. She tried to hide her feelings from Brian, but he saw right through it.

"It will be OK, Libs," he said, hugging her. "I'm here, and I won't let anything happen to you." He wished he felt as confident as he sounded. He decided to sleep on the couch that night, so Libby could feel safe and get some much-needed rest. It was the start of summer, and the next day was sure to be a busy one at the shop.

The nursery and flower shop were booming with business. People were planting flowers and planning weddings, keeping both businesses hopping. Libby was so busy that she didn't have a lot of time to think about the mysterious card. Libby told Brian that she was going to have to hire some seasonal help to keep up with the orders and weekend deliveries. Brian figured that since he didn't work weekends at the paper, and he wanted to spend more time looking out for Libby, he would take the job. Spending more time with her was sweet, but making a little extra income was an added benefit. He told Libby that he would be interested, and before he could get all of the words out of his mouth Libby shouted, "You're hired!" Both of them laughed, which was something that Libby desperately needed to do at that moment.

Brian and Libby had two flower deliveries to make that weekend for two weddings. Both were on Saturday morning, so Brian loaded up the van, and he and Libby headed out to the first delivery at Calvary Baptist Church on Chapel Hill. The air at the church was filled with excitement as bridesmaids giggled and groomsmen bantered, both groups trying to keep the groom from seeing the bride before the wedding.

Brian and Libby walked the flowers to the altar, placing them on either side of the pulpit. When they turned to leave, they found themselves face to face in front of the pulpit. Brian looked at Libby in a way that made her blush, and she scurried off the platform, telling Brian that they had another delivery to do, so there was no time to waste. Brian smiled as he pictured Libby standing face to face with him in a white wedding gown. The thought made his heart skip a beat as he hurried to catch up with her.

The next stop was at St. Matthew's Church on Oak View Lane. This wedding was for a couple who had been given a second chance at happiness after losing their previous spouses to death. The flowers were modest, but Libby made sure they were beautiful sprays that gave off the fragrance of spring. There was no standing on the platform in front of the pulpit this time, but as they headed back down the aisle to the van, Brian grabbed Libby's hand, and they walked quietly side by side to the back of the church. Just holding his hand made Libby's heart flutter. Once again, she felt a blush fill her cheeks and hoped that Brian would not notice. He did, but he didn't remark on it and instead simply tucked the moment away in his memory. He was falling for this girl big time.

After leaving the church, Libby told Brian that they had one more small delivery to make that had come in shortly before they left the shop. It was a last-minute call with an urgent need to deliver a funeral spray of Easter lilies. Libby was unfamiliar with the address, but her GPS indicated that it was not far from St. Matthew's Church. It appeared to be somewhere around the industrial district. With both deliveries made to the churches on time, they set out to find the location of their last order.

The farther they drove, the less Libby recognized the area. The address was taking them to the dockside of town where there were a lot of barges and riverboats delivering fresh seafood and other freshwater items. As they approached their final destination, Libby began to get a dark feeling again. She didn't remember ever delivering to a funeral home on that side of town. The GPS stopped them at the end of a dead-end road.

This can't be correct, Libby thought. She told Brian that she was going to call the shop to verify the address. Jackie, one of the newer teens that Libby had hired to work the front counter, answered the phone. "Jackie, would you mind checking the address on the last order you took before I left the shop this morning?" she asked. "The address I have has led us to a dead-end street." Jackie assured Libby that she had the correct address. Unfortunately, no return phone number was on the receipt for them to call for clarification.

While Libby was on the phone, Brian got out of the van and looked around. He had parked the van in front of a chain held by two small posts that marked the dead end. Beyond the chain was a path that led into a wooded area. As Libby ended her call, Brian motioned for her to get out of the van, and they started down the path toward the grove of trees. "We came all of this way, so we might as well check this out," Brian said.

Just past the trees was a small clearing. They could hear the river beyond the clearing past more trees. As they entered the clearing, they saw a large brown sleeping bag in the center and noticed what looked like two feet sticking out of one end. They both stopped in their tracks. Had they come across someone sleeping in the middle of the clearing, or was it something more sinister? Brian made his way toward the sleeping bag, looking back at Libby. She froze in place. The closer Brian got, the more the feet sticking out of the sleeping bag didn't look human. He grabbed a large stick lying on the ground and used it to pull at the sleeping bag.

The cloth fell away, revealing not a human body but a manikin. Brian turned to Libby with a mixture of confusion and relief, wondering who would put a manikin in a sleeping bag in the middle of a clearing by the river. Libby moved toward Brian, peering around him to get a closer look. Brian bent down to uncover the rest of the manikin. Taped to its chest was a sealed envelope with Libby's name on it.

Brian picked up the envelope, then handed it to Libby, a confused look on his face.

"What is it?" she asked.

"I don't know," Brian replied. "But it's addressed to you." He and Libby were beyond confused.

As she opened the envelope, Brian noted a small makeshift grave marker pushed into the ground beyond the manikin's head. Libby's name was etched onto it.

"Thanks for making my urgent delivery," the card read. "I hope you like the flowers, as I ordered them special for your funeral."

Libby gasped. Brian grabbed the note to read it for himself. She looked around, wondering if whoever sent them on this wild goose chase was standing in the trees watching them. Brian grabbed Libby's hand and pulled her back to the van.

"What's going on?" she asked. Brian shrugged, as he didn't know how to respond, but he knew it was time to involve the police.

"Libby, whoever is doing this knows where you live and knows where you work. We need to go to the police station now."

She couldn't agree more.

Once they arrived at the police station, Libby and Brian met with Detective Wright. He was a fifteen-year veteran on the force who had spent most of his career in Los Angeles as an undercover detective on a special task force setting up stings for drug rings.

On his last case, he and his partner were at a drug house where they had been undercover for about thirteen months. They had been able to penetrate to the top level of the drug ring and were due to meet the kingpin that evening. The plan was to get him into the house. Then the SWAT team would surround the house and arrest everyone, so their cover would remain intact.

The plan was going well, executed with precision. The kingpin arrived, but as he made his way to the porch, another van pulled up, and one of the gang members got out and headed straight toward him. After they exchanged a few words, the kingpin motioned for the man to head back to the van. Then, instead of entering the house, he yelled for the men to come out to meet him. This was not a part of how the police had planned the bust, but they knew that if they didn't comply, it would look suspicious.

Detective Wright and his partner stepped out onto the porch. "What's up, man?" Wright asked in his best gangster voice. "I thought we had business to take care of inside."

"We have some business to take care of, alright," the kingpin replied, "but we can take care of it right here." With that, the kingpin raised his arm and swung it down, then hit the ground. Several men with guns exited the van and began firing.

Detective Wright dove behind the concrete wall of the porch, yelling in his earpiece for backup. The SWAT team swarmed the place within minutes. It didn't take long for the gunfight to end, but in the chaos, the kingpin got away. As Detective Wright stood to survey the scene, he saw at least three men lying in the street. When he turned back toward the house, he found his partner, Dave, lying just inside the front door, having taken a bullet through the head. At that moment, Detective Wright decided enough was enough, and he made the move from Los Angeles to small-town America. He had witnessed enough death and had given too much of his own life, and he wanted a safer and less demanding job.

Detective Wright welcomed Brian and Libby into his office. Visibly shaken, Libby sat in the chair at the front of his desk. He offered her a cola, which she readily accepted. She had missed lunch and felt that her blood sugar was dropping. Libby told him about the card that she had received at her home and the wild goose chase to the river. She wondered if the two were connected and if it could all be a bad joke. She wanted him to tell her that she had nothing to worry about, but her instinct told her that was not true. Sure enough, Wright was certain that this was no joke. He felt that someone was sending a clear warning to Libby, and her life could be in danger. He asked if she could think of anyone who would want to harm her. Initially, Libby could not think of anyone, but as she reflected on the numerous foster homes and sinister situations that she had been in, her mind stopped at James. She hesitated to mention him because he was supposed to be in prison. After a few more minutes of questioning, Detective Wright completed his interview and assured Libby that if he found any leads, he would let her know. He had already decided that his first move would be to call the prison to check on James.

CHAPTER
EIGHT

Brian didn't feel comfortable leaving Libby at home alone, so he convinced her to let him stay at the house. He would take the guest room downstairs, and she would stay upstairs in her room. Brian was not crazy about the fact that having him there overnight might cause gossip in the neighborhood, but he was more concerned about her life than her reputation at that point. Libby also felt much safer with Brian near her.

They drove past Brian's apartment to pick up some clothes and toiletries along with his dog, Scooter. Scooter was a German shepherd that had been with Brian for about five years. He took to Libby quickly, wagging his tail and licking her face and hands. He was friendly, fiercely protective, and loyal. After packing up his clothes and necessities and grabbing some doggie essentials, they picked up some burgers and fries. Neither of them had eaten since breakfast, and Brian's stomach was growling louder than a mad dog.

On the drive to Libby's house, both of them were quiet, unsure of what to think or say. Brian's mind was going in a hundred directions, conjuring various scenarios and outcomes. He would have to cool it, as he didn't want to scare Libby, although he was somewhat frightened himself. The realization hit him that he could not imagine his life without Libby in it. How, in such a short time, had she made her way so deeply into his heart?

After arriving at her home, Brian took Libby's key, unlocked the door, and stepped inside. He made Libby stay in the doorway with Scooter until he could check out the rest of the house. Libby felt a wave of gratefulness toward Brian and was surprised at her strong emotional attachment to him. At that moment, all she wanted was to be held in his strong embrace.

Brian walked through every room in the house, checking closets and ensuring the windows were secure. When he felt certain everything was safe, he allowed Libby and Scooter into the house. Detective Wright had told them that he would have cruisers drive by throughout the night, which made them both feel safer. The idea that anyone would want Libby dead seemed preposterous to her. She couldn't see any reason why someone would want to harm her, except perhaps for James, and he was in prison. Just the thought of James sent chills up her spine as her mind struggled to comprehend the consequences if Brian had not been there for her. If it had not been for him coming to her rescue at the campground, Libby was sure that she would have been scarred for life. She owed Brian a debt of gratitude and wondered how she could ever repay him.

Libby and Brian headed to the living room to eat their food. Scooter lay between them on the couch, his head and paws resting on Libby's lap, eating the occasional scrap that fell from her food wrapper. Scooter had quickly warmed up to Libby, as she had to him.

After a full day and with a full stomach, it didn't take long for Libby to become sleepy. Brian was also starting to yawn. Libby showed him to the guest room and made sure he had an extra blanket and clean towels, then said goodnight and headed up the stairs to her room.

After a hot shower, she brushed her teeth, put on her PJs, and headed to bed. She got three feet into her room and then froze. The hairs on her neck and arms stood up. She knew that something was out of place. She looked around the room, and her eyes stopped at the chest of drawers. The top drawer was slightly open. She walked over to open the drawer and then stopped just short of the knob. She pulled her arm back and turned to leave the room. Something was definitely wrong, and her spirit was warning her to pull back. She needed to get Brian and quickly.

Libby took the steps two at a time and caught Brian just as he was coming out of the kitchen. She felt rather stupid as she explained her fears to Brian and then asked if he would check it out.

Brian looked through Libby's bedroom, checking under her bed and in the closet before heading toward the chest of drawers. His palms were sweating, and his heart was in his throat. Libby was not the only one who felt a sense of dread. As he reached for the drawer, Scooter jumped up and pushed Brian back. That was enough for Brian to call Detective Wright instead of opening the drawer himself.

He, Libby, and Scooter went downstairs to the kitchen to make the call. As soon as Brian picked up the phone, a loud blast shook the house. He and Libby hit the floor as Scooter stood toward the stairs, his hackles raised. Smoke was billowing down the steps as the upstairs smoke detector blared, causing Scooter to bark even louder. Brian dialed 911 as he, Libby, and Scooter exited the house to wait for help. Neither of them uttered a word as they waited in shock for the police to arrive.

Detective Wright and two squad cars pulled up within minutes. Libby and Brian were still outside looking up as smoke rolled out of the shattered bedroom window. Broken glass and shards of wood littered the front lawn. Brian and Libby quickly explained the events leading up to the blast. Wright did a sweep of the perimeter and then sent officers to check the backyard. He called for the bomb squad and waited for them to arrive and check the scene before entering the home.

He pulled Brian aside as Libby stood with Scooter, watching as neighbors came out of their homes to see what all the commotion was about. "Brian, I want to be straight with you," Wright said. "I believe that Libby's life may be in grave danger. I would like for you to stay close to her at all times and let me know if you see or hear anything out of the ordinary. I'm waiting on a call back from the prison about James, but in the meantime, we need to take every precaution." He didn't need to tell Brian to stay close to Libby. A bulldozer could not drag him from her side. Detective Wright informed Brian and Libby that they would need to stay at a motel. He sent one of his officers to follow them and ensure that they arrived safely. The police needed time to secure the house, ascertain what had happened, and gather any possible evidence that could point to a likely culprit. Wright would not even allow Brian to go to his apartment to collect more clothing because he could not be sure that his apartment was not compromised as well. Brian handed his apartment key over to Detective Wright, so the police could do a sweep of his place.

The motel was about five miles away from the Hydes' house. Libby sat in silence for the entire drive, afraid that if she spoke, she would break down in hysterical tears. That was not a sight that Brian would want to see.

By the time they checked into the motel, Libby was utterly exhausted. She and Brian shared adjoining rooms because Brian didn't want to be too far from Libby if she needed him. Once in bed, Libby was out like a light. Brian, on the other hand, found it difficult to fall asleep. His concern for Libby ran deep. He could not remember ever feeling such a strong bond with anyone. He hated the thought of someone taunting and stalking Libby like an animal. Finally, Brian knelt next to his bed, bowed his head, and closed his eyes in prayer. "Lord, I thank you for the protection that you provided for us tonight. Please place a hedge of protection around us. You have placed me in this young woman's life for a reason, and I want to be sensitive to Your leading. Give me insight and discernment, so I may fulfill Your will in this situation. In Jesus's name I pray. Amen."

When Brian finished his prayer, a feeling of peace swept over him. Within minutes of praying, Brian was sound asleep, Scooter lying on the floor beside him.

The next morning, Libby sat up in bed and looked around the motel room, trying to get her bearings. The explosion seemed surreal to her. As she walked through those moments in her mind, she contemplated what would have happened if she or Brian had opened that drawer. One of them could be dead right now or, at the very least, seriously injured. The thought made her physically ill and the realization began to sink in that someone had attempted to cause her great harm or even kill her. Who would do such a thing? She thought about how her parents must have felt with their house on fire as they tried to navigate the smoke-filled home before succumbing to the darkness of death.

She was so deep in her thoughts that she almost missed her

phone ringing. It was Brian. He wanted to know if she would meet him for breakfast in the lobby. She quickly got dressed and then headed to the lobby to meet Brian and Scooter.

The motel, which had been recently remodeled, was very nice. The breakfast buffet offered a variety of cooked as well as cold food choices. Initially, Libby didn't feel hungry, but when she smelled the bacon and eggs, her mouth watered. She was ready to eat. She and Brian loaded up their plates, with Brian adding a little extra for Scooter, since the motel was friendly toward pets. They decided to take their breakfast outside and sit on the patio, so they could speak privately about the previous night's incident.

Scooter sat on the ground next to Brian, chewing on some ham that Brian had tossed down to him while they discussed why anyone would want to kill Libby.

As they were finishing breakfast, Libby's cell phone rang. It was Detective Wright. He told her that the bomb squad had scoured her bedroom and pieced together the remnants of a small pipe bomb. The damage was limited to her bedroom, with the bomb rigged primarily to affect whoever opened the drawer. Clearly, Libby was the intended target. Although this was disturbing to Libby, she was thankful that it was her life that had been targeted and no one else. Libby did not want to call the Hydes for fear they would cut their vacation short, and she really didn't know what to tell them at this time. No, she decided to wait until she had more answers. Wright wanted her and Brian to come to the station to discuss who the culprit could be. The plot was definitely thickening. After Libby filled Brian in on the details, he knew that he would lay down his life to protect her.

Before they left for the police station, Brian excused himself to make a quick call to his pastor to let him know that he would not be at church that evening and that he would explain why later. He asked his pastor to pray for their safety and for wisdom and discernment. If they were going to figure out who was trying to kill Libby, they were going to need more help than the police could give. They needed divine intervention. He also asked his pastor to pray for divine protection for Libby.

When they arrived at the station, Detective Wright took them into his office and shut the door. He proceeded to tell them that

James had been released from prison two weeks earlier. His parents had hired a high-powered attorney who obtained an early release due to a technicality, and James was awaiting a new trial. Detective Wright had called the sheriff's office in James's hometown, and they were going to send out a sheriff's deputy to question him on his whereabouts over the past two weeks. James was looking more and more like their prime suspect.

As Libby recalled her last encounter with him, shivers went down her spine. She knew he was a rapist, but she struggled to wrap her mind around the possibility that he could also be a murderer. His parents were decent people even though they had blinders on when it came to James. While incarcerated, James and his parents had attended weekly family therapy sessions at the prison. His parents were slowly coming to grips with the concept of tough love, but was it too late to save James from becoming a hardened criminal and possibly a murderer?

As Libby and Brian left the police station, Detective Wright did his best to encourage their safety without overly alarming them to the potential danger. If his instincts were correct, Libby would face yet another attempt on her life unless they could catch the responsible party first. He felt that he had not done enough to protect his partner, and he was going to do his level best to protect Libby.

Brian drove Libby home from the police station. They had boarded up her bedroom window, and she was going to stay in the master bedroom, which was closer to the guest room. Brian was still staying at Libby's home with no intention of leaving until the police apprehended the suspect. Libby thought it best not to contact the Hydes because there was no real harm done to the structure of the house, and they deserved to complete their vacation. She didn't want to put an early end to their lifelong dream when there was not a thing they could do by being at home, except to possibly be in harm's way. Besides, Libby had Brian and Scooter as well as the support of the nursery staff, who were handling the business in her absence.

Libby hired a local contractor to repair her room. Beside the chest of drawers, there was only minor damage done, which was repairable with spackle, paint, and a new window. She decided to go with a new paint color in her room since they were going to be painting anyway. It made her feel a little more in control of the situation, even though she knew it was only an illusion.

As she walked around the room, her mind went back to that night. She wondered what had caused her to pause and consider that something was wrong. She recalled feeling as if something or someone was looking out for her and warned her of the impending danger. The thought took her back to her childhood and a verse that she had learned in Sunday school, Jeremiah 29:11: "For I know that plans that I have for you, declares the Lord, plans to prosper you and not to harm you, plans to give you a hope and a future."

CHAPTER
NINE

The next morning, Brian waited to take Libby to work. While working she could focus on the flowers, which were in gorgeous bloom and fragrant, rather than speculate on the possibility of another attempt on her life. Both the nursery and the flower shop were alive with color and smelled heavenly. It was hard to think of death when so much life was blooming around her.

Agnes, the arrangement designer, was teaching Libby how to create flower arrangements. Libby was getting quite good at it, and Agnes said she had a real knack, an artistic flair, and an eye for detail. As Agnes spoke, it brought back memories of what Libby's mother had said to her as they planted flowers along the walk leading to the front door of their house. Little did Agnes know that to Libby arranging the flowers was therapeutic and soothing. The employees at the nursery and flower shop were unaware of the detailed circumstances surrounding Libby as Detective Wright requested the news crew keep the story quiet so as not to alarm the community until they could ascertain if this were just an isolated case. Libby told the employees that there had been an electrical malfunction in the home, which resulted in a small fire, thus the bedroom makeover. She didn't want word to get back to the Hydes that trouble was brewing.

She threw herself into her work, and before long, it was

time for lunch. Time always flew by when Libby was working with flowers.

"I'll have the chicken salad sandwich and chips please," Libby said to the clerk as she and Brian ordered lunch.

"Sounds good. I'll have the same," Brian said. While they waited for their food, they sipped their drinks. "How has your day been?" Brian asked.

"Busy but good," she replied. "I haven't had much time to think over the past few days." Brian agreed that it was good for Libby to stay busy, but he wanted her to spend some time thinking back over her life to see if anyone other than James came to mind who would want to hurt her.

"My parents were killed in a house fire, but it was sometime later before I learned that the police believed it to be arson. Arrests were never made." With this confession to Brian, Libby flashed back to the moment she found out the truth about the fire. It was between the time she was removed from the Thompson's home but had not yet been placed at the Nelson's. She was still living in the shelter assisting the social worker to place the other children who had been removed from the Thompson's home. Libby was adamant that she would not be placed in her next home until the other children had been properly placed in good homes.

Libby remembers that it was a beautiful day. The sun was bright in the sky, and she recalled the laughter of the children as they played in the yard, hearing the birds chirping and singing. It was one of the more tolerable days in the shelter. They were out in the yard when the police car arrived. Just seeing a police car brought angst to her young heart. Within a few moments, the director of the shelter came to the door and called Libby into her office. As she walked back into the building, Libby felt as if a dark cloud were forming above her.

Sitting at the desk was an older gentleman. He looked so serious in his uniform yet had a gentle demur that left her feeling vulnerable. He quickly introduced himself as Detective Lee. He explained that he was placed on the case of the house fire that had killed her parents. Libby's head was spinning as she could not grasp what reason he could have for being here. It was a simple house fire that took her parent's lives, wasn't it?

Seeing the confusion on Libby's face, and wanting to protect her young mind, he spoke with a gentle tone. "Libby, I have been working on your parent's case since the fire marshal determined that the fire that destroyed your home and killed your parents was not an accident." Libby felt that same punch in the gut as she had felt at the Killian's home when the social worker first told her that her parents had died. She felt a bit dizzy as Detective Lee reached out to steady her and help her to sit down. "I am not sure that I understand what you are saying", Libby spoke with trembling lips dreading his response. "Libby, it pains me to have to tell you that the deaths of your parents were not accidental. The fire was arson and your parent's deaths are now listed as homicide. We are actively pursuing leads to who might have done such a thing. Do you understand what I am telling you?"

Libby nearly choked on her words as she responded, "Someone killed my parents?" Detective Lee looked at Libby with such compassion in his eyes. "I am here to ask you if you know of anyone who might have been angry with your parents?" The question reverberated in her mind then and still does today. Recalling that day, tears began to well up in her eyes. She turned to wipe them away before Brian could see her pain.

"Since then, I have been in and out of more than a few bad foster homes," she continued, "but I can't believe that anyone from those homes would try to kill me." Matt's name fleetingly crossed Libby's mind but since his grandmother's case had gone cold, she no longer thought much about Matt. Surely if he had been the one that killed his grandmother, they would have proven it by now.

Brian agreed that it seemed unlikely except for James. He recalled the brutality that James had displayed with Libby. Had Brian not been there, he was sure that James would have raped her without thinking twice. He considered James a serial rapist and a brute when it came to women. Libby still had her doubts that James could do such a thing, but she had to concede that he was the only person who seemed to be a likely suspect. She was glad that Detective Wright was looking into his whereabouts and that Brian was there to protect her. She hated feeling vulnerable.

After lunch, Brian dropped Libby off at the nursery and then headed to the newspaper office.

"I'll pick you up after work, Libs," Brian said. As he drove away, Libby stood there for a moment, grateful that Brian had come back into her life and feeling her connection to him growing stronger each day.

At 7:00 p.m., Libby locked up the nursery and texted Brian to see if he was coming to pick her up. He apologized, saying he had gotten a last-minute assignment, a fire at an abandoned warehouse. He asked if Agnes could drop Libby at home and then stay with her until he arrived. Agnes agreed to drop her off, but she had plans to help her daughter at church preparing for a women's conference, so she couldn't stay. She invited Libby to come with her, but Libby didn't want to leave Scooter at home by himself, as he needed to be let out and fed. Had Agnes known what was going on, she would have insisted. Rather than tell Brian that Agnes could not stay or tell Agnes why Brian wanted her to stay, Libby opted to go home alone. She would have Scooter to keep her company. It was surprising how much having Scooter around comforted her.

As Agnes pulled into Libby's driveway, the sun was just starting to set, and a beautiful ray of light shone on the horizon. Libby took a deep breath, thanked Agnes for the ride, then headed for the door. She could hear Scooter inside the house, barking and growling.

That's odd behavior for Scooter, she thought. He was usually very quiet, so quiet she hardly knew he was around. As she unlocked the door, she heard a loud crash. Initially, she was hesitant to enter the house; however, she could still hear Scooter barking and feared he may have knocked something over. She entered the house and turned on the hall light. She moved toward the barking sound and rounded the corner into the family room just in time to see someone climb out the window with Scooter close behind, barking and growling.

Libby ran back to lock the front door and then dialed 911. She was still on the phone with the 911 operator when her cell phone rang. She glanced down to see that it was Brian. She would have to call him back as soon as the police arrived, and she could hang up her 911 call. The 911 operator continued to make small talk with Libby to keep her calm until help arrived. Libby paced as they spoke, her mind spinning.

The police arrived within five minutes. Libby told them what had happened and showed them the window through which the intruder left. They could tell the lock had been tampered with, and there were fresh footprints beneath the window seal. One of the officers took pictures of the site and then placed a piece of cloth that he found hanging by a nail outside the window into an evidence bag. Apparently, the intruder had gotten caught on the nail in his hurry to leave. The material appeared to be from a plaid cotton shirt, which was nothing significant unless there were traces of DNA on it.

After the officers finished processing the scene, Detective Wright ordered one of the junior officers to remain outside of Libby's house for the rest of the night. When everyone else was gone, Libby pulled out her cell phone to return Brian's call, but it went directly to voicemail. She didn't think much about it, as she knew he was on an important story. She left him a message to call her back as soon as he was able to. She didn't want to frighten him by leaving any details of the intruder. She knew that he would be upset that Agnes was not with her.

It was now 10:30 p.m. Libby did a walk-through of the house, checking each door and window to ensure they were secure. Scooter stayed right beside her. She was seriously considering having an alarm system installed. One of the officers had nailed the window in question shut to prevent anyone from reentering it. Libby peeked out the front window to see the cruiser sitting by the curb, which gave her a modicum of comfort. Finally, she sat down on the couch and waited for Brian to return her call. She could not understand why he had not called back and why he was not already home. She yawned and laid her head back on the couch as she patted Scooter's head. Before she knew it, she was fast asleep.

At 2:00 a.m., Libby awoke, realizing she had fallen asleep while waiting for Brian to call her. She checked her phone to see if there was a missed call or message, which there was not. Then she checked Brian's room to see if perhaps he had come home and didn't want to wake her, but he was not there. Libby wondered where he could be. He hadn't gone into detail about the assignment, but Libby knew it had to be important for him to be away for so long. She tried his cell phone again, but it went straight to voicemail. She didn't leave a message but instead sent him a text. She was trying not to worry, but after everything that had happened over the past three days, it was hard not to. The only thing that she could do was wait with Scooter at her side. Thank goodness she had him.

Libby grabbed a blanket, turned on the television, and once again fell asleep. She awoke to a banner running across the television screen that read "Breaking News."

"Last evening a fire broke out at an abandoned warehouse on Riverfront Drive," a reporter said. "From what we can tell, the cause has been determined to be arson." Libby listened to the reporter describe how the building had collapsed on two reporters who were covering the story, which caused Libby's ears to perk up. The police located the body of reporter Angela Martin, but as of airtime, the police had not yet located the second reporter.

Libby's heart raced as she dialed Brian's number again. It went straight to voicemail. In a panic, she jumped up and turned to run to the hallway to get her car keys, but her feet got tangled in the blanket, and she fell hard against the coffee table, hitting her head. As Libby lost consciousness, Scooter stood by, whimpering and licking her face.

CHAPTER
TEN

A s her eyes fluttered open, Libby could tell it was dark, though she was unsure what time it was or where she was. She could see the moon shining through the trees and the fog rolling across the meadow. She was lying on the ground, her clothes moist from the dew. Slowly, she sat up, dazed and confused. Her head hurt as she held her palm against her left temple. It was sore. As the memory of the past three days came crashing back into her mind, she slouched to the ground, sobbing so hard that her entire body was shaking, the painful memories sweeping over her in waves. It seemed as though hours passed before she was able to stand. She looked around, trying to iden-tify where she was and wondering how she had gotten there and why she was in such a strange place.

Libby took a step forward, then two steps. Then she ran past the edge of the woods and into a clearing where the moon was full and shining brightly, as if a light had been turned on in the night sky. Turning a full circle, she looked for anything that would help her understand where she was. As Libby stumbled forward, she felt a heaviness that would not lift, its weight so oppressive that it felt as if it were going to crush the breath out of her. She tried to shake the feeling as her mind reeled with a jumble of thoughts. The grass beneath her feet was soft and wet. That was when she realized she was barefoot. The rain was falling gently, and the odor of fragrant flowers wafted into her nostrils. How could such a sweet fragrance enter the bitterness growing in her heart? Would the bitterness take hold or dissipate under the dread that was consuming her?

Without knowing why, Libby fell to her knees and began to pray, but the words would not come, as she didn't know how or what to pray.

In the midst of her struggle, she heard a soft voice call her name. She thought that, in her feeling of helplessness, she was hearing things, but then she heard it again. She stood up and cocked her head to the side, listening intently.

"Libby, come here," the voice said. It didn't scare her but gave her a feeling of security. She followed the sound, which was coming from alongside the river's edge. When she was within a few feet of the river, the voice told her to stop. "Look up," the voice said. Libby raised her head and looked up and across the river. Thousands of stars were adorning the night sky, but it was the moon that drew her attention as it shone brightly over a small farmhouse. "Go, Libby," the voice instructed. By then Libby was beyond questioning. Her head hurt, her feet were cold, and fatigue was setting in, so when she saw the bridge leading across the river toward the farmhouse, she didn't hesitate to cross it.

It took about twenty minutes for Libby to reach the farmhouse. It was more of a cottage, and it appeared to be from the early 1900s. The brick was crumbling, and the shutters were peeling. Moss and ivy were growing along the wall, and the brush was somewhat overgrown. A small picket fence surrounded the front yard.

As she passed through the gate and drew closer to the house, Libby saw a faint light through the window. The closer she got to the window, the brighter the light became. The feeling of panic and dread began to lift as if a huge weight she had been carrying was lifted.

Wondering where she was and whom the house belonged to, she peered through the window. Inside was a small desk upon which sat a lamp and an open book. She noted how sparse the furnishings were.

"Go read," the voice whispered. The door creaked as it swung open and bid her to enter.

It was warm and comfortable inside. Libby immediately felt at ease.

"Sit and read, Libby."

Libby sat at the desk, pulling the book toward her. She recognized it as a Bible. Libby had quit reading the Bible long ago. Not many of her foster homes were conducive to Christianity, and ever since her parents' death, she had felt angry with God and didn't have any desire to read the Bible. However, as she pulled the Bible toward her, she felt an awakening in her soul as if she were being reunited with an old friend.

As a child, Libby's family attended church faithfully. She loved Sunday school and all the Bible stories and characters. Her teacher told the stories in a way that made the characters come to life. She would often wonder how young David could slay a giant or how a big fish could swallow a man, but Libby loved her teacher and wanted to believe that what she was telling her was true.

Each summer she would go to vacation Bible school. Her parents would take her along as they decorated the church. Every year was a new theme with new decorations. It was so much fun watching them transform the church into a space station or a submarine. Her heart longed to be back in those days, mostly because her parents were there, alive and happy.

Libby's father had been an elder in the church, and she was used to tag along when he would go on visitation. She met many new kids as her father went to different homes. She would play with the children as her father talked with the parents. She often wondered what he was talking to them about. Some parents appeared happy to hear what her father was saying. Others would thank him for his time but say they were not interested and send him and Libby on their way. She knew the conversations must be serious because sometimes the women, and even the men, would cry. Then her father would pray with them. After prayer, they all seemed to light up and be full of joy. Her dad would always leave his business card in case they needed to talk with him. He would also invite them to church. The visits were always somewhat of a mystery to Libby.

"Read," the voice persisted. Libby picked up the Bible and began to read the Gospel of John.

"In the beginning was the Word and the Word was with God and the Word was God. He was with God in the beginning and through Him, all things were made. Without Him, nothing was made that has been made. In Him was life and that life was the light of all mankind. The Light shines in the darkness and the darkness has not overcome it."

Libby thought about the brightness of the moon as she read the following line: "The Word became flesh and made His dwelling place among us. We have seen His glory, the glory of the one and only Son who came from the Father full of grace and truth."

As she read those words, it brought back memories of the Bible stories and songs that her mother would teach her at bedtime. "This little light of mine, I'm gonna let it shine. Won't let Satan snuff it out, I'm gonna let it shine, let it shine, let it shine, let it shine." She was overcome by a strong feeling of nostalgia. She missed her parents so much. Why did they have to die? Why would anyone want to kill them? They were good people who loved and served the Lord and His church. Then a thought struck her. *Why would anyone want to kill me?* Could there be a connection between her parents' death and the attempt on her life? So many years had passed, but it was still a possibility. However, if so, why?

Her eyes drifted back to the Scripture. "For God so loved the world that He gave His only begotten Son that whosoever believes in Him shall not perish but have eternal life. For God didn't send His Son into the world to condemn the world, but to save the world through Him."

Libby tried to continue reading, but her eyelids became so heavy that she had to lay her head on the desk. Before long, Libby was sound asleep.

It seemed as only minutes passed when Libby felt a hand on her arm.

"Libby, can you hear me?"

She opened her eyes and shut them again, as there was such a bright light.

"Libby, can you hear me?" She recognized the voice this time.

"Is that you, Brian?" she asked.

"Libby, can you open your eyes?" This time the voice was not Brian's; it was a more authoritative voice. She slowly opened her eyes and let them adjust to the light. As her vision became clearer, she saw a doctor standing over her. She turned her head to the side, and there he was.

"Brian, is that really you?" she asked.

"Yes," he replied. "It's me."

As she turned her head, she winced in pain. "My head hurts. Where am I?"

"In the hospital," Brian replied. "You've been here for three days, in a coma."

Libby was stunned. "What happened?" she whimpered.

"I called to tell you that I was going to be working late covering an abandoned warehouse fire," Brian explained. "When we arrived on the scene, the firefighters and police were already there. We got as close to the building as the police would allow us. Angela was pushing forward, asking the officers a million questions, but all they would say was, 'No comment.'

"We walked around the perimeter of the building, looking for more information. On the backside of the warehouse was a door, and no police were around. Angela started toward the door. I told her to stop, but she wouldn't listen. I refused to enter with her, so she asked her partner, Paul, to grab my camera and follow her in. Paul took my camera and my camera bag, and they both disappeared into the building."

"I didn't realize until I went to call you again that my cell phone was still in the camera bag. I went back around to the front of the warehouse to watch along with the other spectators as the fire raged. We stood there for hours.

"Toward morning as the firefighters were sifting through the debris, I overheard one of them tell the officer that it appeared as if someone had planted several pipe bombs in the building. When I heard that, I thought of you. I flagged down a passing car and got a lift back to your house. That's when I found you lying on the floor. Your head was bleeding, and I could not rouse you, so I called 911 for an ambulance. You have been here at the hospital in a coma for the past three days."

Although Libby had a large bump on her left temple, the injury didn't justify her coma. The doctors could not understand why she was not responding. The MRI and CT scans came back normal, and there was no logical reason for Libby not to wake up. It was as if Libby's body was there, but Libby was gone. All they could do was wait and hope that, with time, she would wake up.

"Brian never left her side. He had called Jackie to keep Scooter, which she readily agreed to do, so he could remain with Libby. He was fearful that he would lose Libby without having had the chance to tell her that he loved her and, more importantly, how much God loved her. He was not going to let that happen again.

"Libby, when the doctors couldn't explain why you weren't waking up, I feared that I would never see you again, never be able to talk with you again, and I couldn't imagine my life without you. Libby, I love you."

At those words, Libby began to smile and cry simultaneously. "I love you too, Brian," she whispered. "I love you too." Then she drifted off to sleep.

The next morning, Libby woke early. She had less pain in her head, and she was ferociously hungry. Brian, who was still at her bedside, called the dietary department and ordered her breakfast. Within a few minutes, there was a tray in front of her, laden with biscuits and gravy, hash browns, and bacon. She immediately began to eat. Then, without knowing why, she stopped and asked Brian to bless the meal. A bit taken back by her request, he eagerly prayed a blessing over the food and over Libby. As she began to eat again, she told Brian about her dream and how incredibly real it had felt.

CHAPTER
ELEVEN

After Libby was released from the hospital, Detective Wright asked her to come to the station. She hoped he had some leads to discuss. After her hospital discharge, Libby and Brian discussed Libby's dream experience and the revelation that whoever killed her parents could be the same person that wanted her dead. The question was who and why?

When Libby and Brian arrived, Detective Wright met with them in his office, the door closed. Detective Wright told them that he had done a little research on Libby's past and found out that before her parents died, her father had found evidence that the treasurer of their church had been embezzling funds over a ten-year period, stealing close to $736,000. Libby's father had confronted the treasurer and gave him the chance to go to the pastor and confess. Libby's mother convinced her father that he needed to get his evidence together and put it in a safe place. He did as she advised and put it in the safe at this office. After his death, one of his managers found the file. When he realized what he had found, he took it to the police. The treasurer, Nathan Dillard, was arrested and spent eight years in prison for his crime. He had been released approximately two months earlier. Upon hearing Libby and Brian's theory about her parents' murder and the possibility that the same person could be stalking her, Detective Wright decided it was time to investigate Nathan Dillard.

Nathan was thirty-four years old and married with one daughter at the time Libby's parents knew him. Libby remembered his daughter, Abigail, as they used to play together while their parents were at church meetings. She was a year younger than Libby.

Nathan's wife, Kimberly, liked nice things, and she had convinced Nathan that they needed to move into an affluent neighborhood where the homes were quite expensive. Nathan always did his best to please his wife, so they bought a home in a gated community nicknamed "Snob Knob." They belonged to the local country club, and Kimberly made sure that she was a part of the most influential committees and organizations. She was creating quite a name for herself in the most desirable social clubs. They took Abigail out of the public school and placed her in a private school, another expensive venture. Kimberly bought only brand-name clothing and flaunted her affluence at church. The pressure was on Nathan to keep Kimberly in a style that she was accustomed to, which led to his embezzling from the church, as his paycheck was not cutting it.

When he was tried and convicted, Kimberly, who was embarrassed and humiliated, filed for divorce and retained sole custody of Abigail, moving far away. Within two years she had married a physician from Seattle, Washington, who was able to provide her with the finer things in life. Nathan blamed Libby's family for ruining his life. He didn't display any shock or surprise upon hearing of the death of Libby's parents. No one suspected that he might have had anything to do with the arson, so Detective Wright was beginning to think he had another person of interest in Libby's case.

Brian and Libby left the police station with more questions than answers. Brian told Libby that he wanted to take her somewhere special to get her mind off the case for a while. It was a beautiful day. The sky was clear and blue, and the sun was shining, a balmy breeze in the air.

Brian drove Libby out of town to a small wooded area. He pulled over and asked if she felt up to walking the trails. Wanting to get her mind off her troubles for a while, she readily agreed.

Scooter led the way down the trail while Brian and Libby walked hand in hand. She could not describe the immense feeling of warmth and security she felt just holding Brian's hand. She wondered where their romance would lead.

"Libs?"

"Yes," she replied.

"When you were in the hospital, I thought I might not ever get to speak with you again. There were so many things that I hadn't said to you that I needed to, important things. I prayed like I have never prayed before that God would give me the chance to tell you about His Son, Jesus.

"Libby, I love you, and I want to spend the rest of my life with you, but I'm a Christian first, and my life is dedicated to the Lord."

It was at that moment that the trees opened into the clearing. As they stepped out of the trees, the sun warmed their bodies, and Libby felt a strange sense of familiarity, like déjà vu.

Brian held her hand tightly and kept walking toward the river. "When I was sixteen years old, I was at a youth group meeting at our church," he said. "The youth leaders were talking to a small group of us about sin and its effect on our lives. It was a dismal conversation until they shared about God's holiness and His love toward us. That night our youth leaders introduced us to our Savior and Lord, Jesus Christ. Not everyone was as affected by that discussion as I was, so I was afraid to speak out in the group because I didn't want anyone to poke fun at me. After the meeting ended, I went to one of our leaders, Jason, and asked if we could talk privately."

Jason took Brian to one of the classrooms, shut the door, then sat down with him. Sensing that Brian had been touched by the discussion, Jason asked if he felt convicted. Up until that point, Brian didn't understand what conviction was or if that was what he was feeling.

"I asked him what he meant and what I should do about it," Brian said. "He explained that sin separates us from God, who is holy, and that because of our sin, we are God's enemies. Jason also told me that conviction comes from the Holy Spirit to show us that we are sinners and that we need a Savior."

"He could see that I was confused at how God could love me if I was His enemy, so he explained that because God loved me, He sent His perfect Son, Jesus Christ, who knew no sin, to die for my sin so that I could have eternal life."

"At that moment I felt the gravity of my sin and what it cost God. I bowed my head, confessed to God that I was a sinner, and told Him how sorry I was for my sin. I told Him that I believed that Jesus came to die for me and that I wanted to accept Him as my Savior."

As Brian told the story, Libby remembered the verse in John 3:16, "For God so loved the world that He gave His only begotten Son that whosoever believes in Him should not perish but have eternal life." At that moment, Libby realized what had attracted her to Brian from the moment she met him. Brian exuded a feeling of peace and contentment that came from knowing Christ as his Savior.

Libby wanted so badly to know that peace as well. With tears in her eyes, she turned to Brian. "I want to know that peace, Brian. I want Jesus as my Savior and Lord."

"Libby," Brian replied, "I don't want you to accept Christ as your Savior because you're afraid of losing me but because you realize your need for a Savior, and you're willing to recognize him as your Lord."

Right there in the clearing, Libby and Brian knelt together as Libby called out to God. She humbled herself before the Lord, and He exalted her in His Son, Jesus Christ. When Libby stood up, she was a new creature. The peace she felt was beyond description. She and Brian were both in tears, praising God for His loving-kindness toward them. They took a moment to bask in God's grace before continuing.

Brian and Libby continued hand in hand walking toward the river. Everything was different, and the excitement of their life in Christ together was now the topic of conversation. As they approached the river, Libby once again felt déjà vu. Suddenly, she heard a soft voice speak.

"Libby, look up."

She looked up and saw the bright sun high in the sky, shining down on a small farmhouse across the river.

"Libby, come," the voice commanded.

Without uttering a word, Libby walked toward the bridge, with Brian quietly following, not asking any questions.

It took about twenty minutes for them to reach the farmhouse, the same farmhouse from her dream. Once at the house, Libby stopped, somewhat dazed. "I've been here before," she said softly.

"When?" Brian asked.

"Two days ago."

Brian laughed. "Libs, you were in the hospital two days ago."

She looked at Brian with searching eyes. "I can't explain it, but when we get to the window, you will see a small desk inside with a lamp and a book. Go look."

Brian walked to the window and peered in. The sun was bright, so he cupped his hands around his eyes against the window. Sure enough, there was a small desk with a lamp and a book.

"The door will be open," Libby said, "and you'll see that the book is a Bible, and it will be opened to the Gospel of John. I left off at John 3:16."

Brian was intrigued as they made their way inside, hand in hand.

Brian approached the desk and picked up the Bible, seeing that John 3:16 was underlined. He gasped. "How can this be possible?"

Libby began to piece together what had happened the night that Brian didn't return home. "I remember the next morning, after you didn't come home, hearing the anchorman on TV speaking about the warehouse fire and that two reporters had perished in the flames." Her voice became a hushed whisper, her eyes brimming with tears. "I thought you were dead." Libby remembered jumping up to grab her keys, then everything went black.

"That must have been when you fell," Brian remarked.

Libby and Brian stood there looking at each other for a few minutes before Brian broke the silence. "Libs, I think the Lord has been working toward this moment for some time. He must have something special in store for you. Just continue to trust Him and obey, and I'll stand beside you all the way."

CHAPTER
TWELVE

Five minutes passed without a word. Just as they were about to leave, Nathan Dillard barged through the door. Libby recognized him immediately. Although he was older, he still had the same blue eyes and crew-cut hair.

"How nice of you to make this easy on me," he sneered.

Brian stepped in front of Libby to shield her. "What do you want from us?"

"I don't want anything from you, but I want to exact my revenge on her!" Nathan yelled. That was when Brian saw the gun in Nathan's hand. He made sure to stay between it and Libby. Brian's mind was racing, but God brought him a sense of peace that, no matter the circumstance, the Lord was with them, and Libby was now His child. The verse "Perfect love casts out all fear" came to Brian's mind.

At that moment, Libby stepped out from behind Brian to address Nathan. "Hello, Mr. Dillard," she said with a calmness in her voice that shook him. Nathan could not believe that she recognized him after all these years. The last time he saw her she was just a child. "How are you?" she asked.

"Why should you care how I'm doing?" he replied. "I lost my home, my family, and my dignity, and I've spent over eight years in prison because of your family."

"What do you want from Libby?" Brian asked, careful not to

insinuate himself into the question again.

"I plan to take care of some unfinished business," Nathan replied. "You were all supposed to be home! I made special arrangements to discuss my situation with your father. I told him that I would bring Abigail with me, so I could be sure that you were all there."

As he spoke, Libby realized Nathan was about to admit to murdering her parents and that he had intended her to die with them as well. Initially, rage began to build within her. She was facing the man who had killed her parents and who, apparently, had been trying to kill her. Because of him, she spent eight years in the foster-care system, enduring more abuse than any child should have to. They had both spent the last eight years in a prison, but his was deserved. She was just about to spew hateful words at him when she heard a still, soft voice in her mind. *Libby, he needs to know your Savior. Introduce him to your Savior.* Libby took a deep breath and found an inner strength that she didn't know she had.

"Mr. Dillard, do you remember when you used to take Abigail and I to the church playground and push us on the swings?" Nathan appeared to be thrown off by Libby's question. "You would play tetherball with us and let the ball come around and hit you in the head, then fall to the ground as if you were hurt," she continued. "When we came over to see if you were OK, you would grab us and become the tickle monster, chasing us around the playground."

As her words washed over him, the memories came flooding back. He had spent so much time being angry about losing his wife and daughter that he hadn't taken the time to remember how much love they had shared.

"You were our vacation Bible school teacher the summer before my parents died. I can still remember the lesson. You were teaching us about the crucifixion and resurrection of Jesus." She went on to recount how Mr. Dillard told them about the scourging of Jesus and the nailing of his hands and feet to the cross. He had told the story so matter of fact, without emotion. As a child, she had asked Mr. Dillard, "If Jesus is God, why didn't He just go back to heaven instead of letting them beat Him? You taught us that Jesus endured the pain and suffering because He loved us. You said He loved us so much that He spread out his arms and died."

Nathan teared up as he remembered his nightly routine with Abigail. "Daddy, how much do you love me?" she would ask.

"This much," he would reply, stretching his arms out as far as he could. Then Abigail would run into them as he hugged her tight. Mr. Dillard was starting to realize he had never really understood God's love for him, so much that He would allow His son to die.

Mr. Dillard was deep in his memories when Libby began singing softly. "Amazing grace, how sweet the sound..."

Without skipping a beat, Brian joined in.

That saved a wretch like me.
I once was lost, but now am found;
was blind, but now, I see.

Through many dangers toils, and snares,
I have already come.
'Tis grace that brought me safe thus far,
and grace will lead me home.

The Lord has promised good to me,
His word my hope secures;
He will my shield and portion be,
As long as life endures.

As they finished singing, Nathan dropped to his knees, and Libby knelt beside him, her arm around his shoulder.

"My God, Libby, what have I done?" he sobbed. As Libby held him, Brian prayed. When his crying slowed, Nathan stood, and Libby led him over to the desk to sit, his gun still lying on the floor where he had dropped it. "Libby, can you ever forgive me?" he asked.

"Mr. Dillard, I already have, but even more importantly, so has God."

He began sobbing again, laying his head on the Bible. Brian and Libby stood behind him, their hands on his shoulders as they silently prayed for God to heal him.

When Nathan raised his head from the Bible, he was a new creature in Christ, a child of God.

At the police station, Detective Wright led Libby, Brian, and Nathan into his office. "What can I do for you?" Detective Wright asked.

"This is Mr. Nathan Dillard," Libby said, "and he has something to tell you."

Nathan confessed to killing Libby's parents as well as attempting to kill Libby. Detective Wright was stunned as, each time Nathan broke down, Libby would comfort and encourage him.

When Nathan was finished speaking, Detective Wright called an officer in to book him. Nathan and Libby hugged before the officer led him out of the room.

After the door shut behind them, Detective Wright looked at Libby, flabbergasted. "What just happened here?" he asked. Brian and Libby relayed the entire story to him. When they finished, Detective Wright shook his head in wonder. "That must be some God you have."

"Indeed!" Libby replied. "Would you like to meet him?" She looked at Brian and smiled.

Nathan's trial didn't last long due to his full confession and cooperation with the police. Libby told the jury that Nathan had asked forgiveness, which she had gladly given, and she asked for the court to be merciful. Touched by Libby's request, the jury recommended thirty years, including time served. That meant Nathan could be released in as early as ten years for good behavior. Libby and Brian promised they would visit him once a week for Bible study and be there when he went before the parole board to stand on his behalf. Her forgiveness amazed Nathan, but knowing God had forgiven him made him more focused on getting his life right, so he could live for the Lord and serve Him whether in or out of prison.

CHAPTER
THIRTEEN

With that chapter of Libby's life closed, she looked forward to what her life in the Lord would bring. Brian had been working overtime at the paper. His new position brought many challenges and additional responsibilities. She missed their long walks, holding hands and laughing as they watched Scooter chase a squirrel or simply chase his tail.

As Indian summer approached, it was beautiful driving through the country. The flowering trees were in full bloom, and color splashed across the horizon with hues of yellow, pink, and green. It was at that time of year that she missed her folks the most, remembering their camping trips and hikes in the forest. If time healed the hurt from loss, she wondered how much time it would take, as her heart ached almost as much now as it had when they died. It had been a few years since Libby had been to the gravesite. Perhaps it was time to plan a trip back there before she headed to college.

Mr. and Mrs. Hyde were due to arrive back in the States in less than a week. Libby could not wait to meet them at the airport. She had so much to tell them, as she was sure they would have to tell her. She was surprised at how much she missed having them around. Business was booming, and they had a few new contracts that Libby had picked up over the summer. She also had to hire someone to replace Brian, as his promotion kept him too busy at the paper to work a side job.

They had planned to pick the Hydes up at the airport together just as they had dropped them off, but Brian was unsure that he could make it due to a new assignment at the paper that was hush-hush. She thought for sure that Brian would share it with her, as he had all his other assignments, and she was somewhat hurt that he would not. Perhaps he was losing interest in her. The thought made her cringe, and she tried to push it from her mind. She was almost sure that Brian was the man the Lord had for her.

Ever since accepting Christ as her Savior and Lord, she had been praying about her relationship with Brian. She always felt a peace about it, and she was trying her best to trust the Lord in her new walk as a Christian. *I wonder if Brian prays about our relationship,* she thought. In all of their conversations, they had not broached the subject of where the relationship was taking them. Perhaps it was time.

Church was a wonderful experience for Libby. Brian's pastor, Stan Ward, was a middle-aged man, married with three children. He had a calm and quiet demeanor, but when he stood in the pulpit, he transformed and preached with passion and authority. Libby was like a sponge, soaking up as much of the Word as she could.

Of Pastor Ward's three children, their twin twelve-year-old boys, Bray and Clay, were in middle school, and their sixteen-year-old daughter, Vanessa, was in high school. Libby helped with the youth group, so she soon became good friends with all of them. Pastor Ward's wife, Linda, worked as a secretary at the high school, so she could be off during the summer with her children. Any chance that she could, Libby would attend home Bible studies to get to know some of the women of the church a little better. She remembered going with her mother to the many showers, dedications, and Bible studies that the women were involved in. Her new church reminded her of the church she grew up in, and she didn't realize how much she had missed the Christian fellowship.

Two days were left before the Hydes would arrive. Libby made sure that the house was clean, the yard mowed, and the garden alive with color, so when they reached home, they would be able to just sit, relax, and share their adventurous stories. She had not heard from Brian since Sunday at church, so she called to verify that he was still intending to go with her to the airport. He didn't answer his phone, so Libby left a message for him to contact her as soon as possible. She closed the shop and headed home. When she arrived at the house, she was impressed at how beautiful the flowers and plants along the walk looked. Once again, memories of the time spent with her mother gardening came flooding back, sending a tear rolling down her cheek.

"Lord," she whispered, "help me be the kind of Christian that my parents were."

She parked her car, checked the mailbox, and unlocked the front door. She immediately saw the answering machine blinking with messages. The first message was from the Hydes, letting Libby know their flight number and time of arrival. The next message was from Linda Ward, wanting to know if Libby needed any last-minute help preparing for the Hydes' arrival. Libby had given her a key, as she was going to drop off some meals that the women of the church had prepared, so the Hydes would not have to worry about cooking for a few days. The third message was from Brian, letting Libby know that he would not be able to make it to the airport because of an out-of-town assignment and would not be back until sometime next week.

Libby wondered why he had not called her cell. He had been so secretive as of late, and the thought crossed her mind that he had found another woman. She quickly shook off that notion and tried to recall the last time that she spoke with Brian. He seemed a bit apprehensive and evasive when she brought up the subject of picking up the Hydes. Did he know then that he was not going to make it but didn't want to tell her, so he would not have to explain? Libby wanted to trust Brian because she loved him, and if she intended to build a life with him, the relationship needed a base of mutual trust. She mused over the possibility that he didn't trust her. Over the past few months, his behavior had been a bit cagey. Again, she pushed the uncomfortable thoughts out of her mind and focused on the building excitement of having the Hydes back home.

Saturday arrived, and Libby was up early, unable to sleep in anticipation of seeing the Hydes. In her mind, she ran through the list of everything that she wanted to have ready. Linda had the house key, Shelly was covering the nursery and flower shop, the beds all had fresh linens, and there were fresh flowers on every table in the house, which made it smell heavenly. She quickly showered and dressed, then headed for the coffee pot.

The morning paper was on the front step, and she could hear the birds outside chirping and singing. It was as if they knew the Hydes were returning and were happy as well. She ran to the mirror for one last look, grabbed her cell phone and keys, and dashed out the door.

The drive to the airport took about thirty minutes. It was just enough time for Libby's mind to wander to Brian. He had been so ambiguous lately. The only time they had seen each other for the past two weeks was at church, and with so many people around, she didn't have a chance to ask him what was going on. She wished she didn't always think the worst, but her past made it difficult not to. Even being young in the Lord, she knew that was not a proper way to think. She quickly changed her thoughts to the Hydes. Her heart was pounding in anticipation.

She parked in the airport pickup lot and headed to the terminal waiting area. She saw the plane land, and each minute she waited felt like an eternity. Scanning the crowd, she finally saw them come through the doorway. She waved and then ran to meet them.

As she hugged them, she was overwhelmed with love and appreciation.

"Libby, you look wonderful," Mrs. Hyde said.

"I cut my hair and added a few highlights," Libby replied.

"How are things at the nursery and shop?" Mr. Hyde asked.

"There'll be plenty of time to talk later about the business," his wife said. "I want to catch up on more personal things!"

The ride home was full of conversation and laughter. Mr. Hyde drove while Mrs. Hyde showed Libby pictures of the many places they had been and recounted their exploits. Libby grinned from ear to ear, so happy that they were able to have the summer together abroad.

They were so busy chatting when they arrived at the house that Libby was oblivious to the many cars lining the street. Mr. Hyde opened the garage door and pulled in, closing it behind him. Mrs. Hyde was still showing Libby pictures when Mr. Hyde interrupted. "OK, girls, it's time to wrap this up and head inside. There'll be plenty of time to go through all those pictures. I'm ready for some grilling. Libby, I hope you bought some steak!"

As Libby helped them carry their luggage inside, Mr. Hyde finally asked the obvious. "Where's that fellow of yours?"

Libby looked at him and, without planning to, began to cry. Mr. Hyde put down the suitcase he was carrying and embraced her. "I'm so sorry," Libby apologized. "This is your first night home, and I think I'm just a little emotional. Let's get inside and start the grill."

They headed through the door and into the kitchen. It was clear that Linda had been there because dishes of food lined the cabinet and kitchen island.

Wow, Libby thought. *There's enough here to feed an army.*

She walked over to the sink, grabbed a towel, and wiped her face, so the Hydes wouldn't notice her tears. When she turned around though, the Hydes were nowhere in sight. She assumed they had headed to their room to drop off their suitcases, so she opened the refrigerator, grabbed the steaks and supplies, and headed for the back door, planning to get the grill started and surprise them.

When Libby stepped out the door and rounded the corner toward the grill, her jaw dropped.

"Surprise!"

She blushed, thinking they were there to surprise the Hydes but then quickly realized the Hydes were in the crowd as well. Libby was dumbfounded.

"What's going on?" she asked. It was then that Brian stepped forward, got down on one knee, and produced a beautiful diamond ring.

"Libby, I have loved you since the first time I laid eyes on you. Will you be my wife?"

Libby began shaking so hard that she would have dropped the platter of steaks if Mr. Hyde had not scooped it out of her hands. "Brian, I don't understand. I thought you were out of town."

Brian smiled, and Pastor Ward, who was also there, laughed.

"Dear, sweet Libby," Linda quipped, "we've been planning this for the past few weeks."

"But how did you know about it?" Libby asked, turning to the Hydes.

"Brian called us a few weeks back and asked permission to marry you, so we thought we would surprise you," Mrs. Hyde said. "Surprise!"

Libby turned to Brian, tears brimming her eyes. "You didn't answer my question, Libs. Will you marry me?" All eyes were on Libby.

"Of course I'll marry you!" Libby cried. His question answered, Brian placed the ring on her finger and stood up as Libby jumped into his arms.

"I'm hungry," Mr. Hyde said. "Let's fire up that grill!"

Made in the USA
Middletown, DE
11 February 2023

24485327R00066